The Eridanos Library

Hans Erich Nossack

AN OFFERING FOR
THE DEAD

Translated from German by
JOACHIM NEUGROSCHEL

The Eridanos Library
MARSILIO PUBLISHERS

Original German title *Nekyia: Bericht eines Überlebenden*

Copyright © 1947 by Hans Erich Nossack
All rights reserved by Suhrkamp Verlag, Frankfurt am main.

Translation copyright © 1992 by Joachim Neugroschel

Of the present edition copyright © 1992 by
Marsilio Publishers, Corp., 853 Broadway, Suite 1509
New York, New York 10003
All rights reserved.

Distributed in the U.S.A. by Rizzoli International
300 Park Avenue South
New York, New York 10010

The publication of this book wasmade possible in part through a
generous grant from InterNationes.

CLOTH ISBN: 0-941419-29-0
PAPER ISBN: 0-941419-28-2
LOC 90-85935

First edition
MANUFACTURED IN THE UNITED STATES OF AMERICA

An Offering for the Dead

Post amorem omne animal triste.

It was raining again. Or still. I had no power over it.

So I stood up and went back. I told the people: "I will find a road." Not that they asked me to do so. They were lying around like lumps of clay; a few rolled over, sighing. I only said it because at that moment it struck me as the right thing for them. But it was a lie; for I knew that the road could not possibly be where I was heading. And that was why I hesitated after a few steps; perhaps I would have done better to add: "If I do not come back, start off as fast as possible in the opposite direction." I could also have left them something of mine, to reveal that I could no longer be counted on. But I had already vanished behind the curtain of rain. Besides, my words would have made no sense. The people had no inkling whatsoever that I was returning. They had lost all sense of direction.

So I went back to the city. It was a big city.

And I came back. Yes, I am standing among the same people again. It is possible that they did not even notice my absence; for they are still lying there and appear to be sleeping. I looked at them to see whether there was anyone to whom I could tell everything. But I found no one. So I will not speak to them.

Nor will I speak to myself as I did earlier. I used to pace up and down for whole nights, talking to myself. At that time, I had a name with which I did not agree. But now it is different.

One can hardly assume that books will ever again be printed as we were accustomed to seeing. And there will be hardly any readers who would be interested. But throughout these events, which I would like to speak about, I have been haunted by some utterly irrational verses, which I must have once heard somewhere or other:

> Why were we ever granted a voice,
> If we do not also sing by the abyss? When
> Was a voice ever lost then?

I have forgotten the last line. I tried to reconstruct it with the aid of the rhyme; for that last line might perhaps enlighten me about what these verses have to do with me, and in what way they were a kind of help. You see, now I might almost assume that I would have perished without those verses. They virtually immunized me against the events, so that I never fully participated in them, and they found no weak point. Indeed, those verses must have served as a cloak of invisibility. In any case, I cannot find the last line.

I speak to a being that I believe will be here some day. I have the certainty that this is not only a morbid wish to flee my loneliness among the helpless sleepers. At times, the figure of this being stands quite clearly in front of me, and I name it: You. Yes, I want to address it as "You"; it is then at its most visible. But then I promptly start doubting whether it is not just an image drifting up from my memory, from what lies behind me and must be regarded as lost for good. An image that wants to just barely live a bit longer and is therefore trying to attract me. In this way, you see, we are surrounded by dangers.

Is it a friend or a woman? If it is a friend, then the situation is such that one visits him in the evening, when darkness falls. He has not yet lit the light. He has mulled over something in the twilight of his room. Oh, it is you, he says, and one instantly feels one is intruding. And even though one really ought to leave, one remains all the same and sits down with him. A few indifferent words are exchanged, about the weather, about events of the day, or what not. One has to make an effort to find something new to keep the conversation afloat. Why does he not turn on a light? That would make everything much easier. But he apparently wants to stay all by himself. Eventually, one gives up, and the two of you merely sit together. Meanwhile, it has become fully dark. One no longer sees the friend, but this simply makes his presence more and more palpable, yes, and gradually so tormenting that one scarcely dares to breathe, and there seems to be too little room for a second person here. So one has no choice but to become completely one with the other. This other sits facing the window. The curtains have not been drawn. He gazes at Orion, which is in the sky. It must be winter. He gazes precisely at the place where the great nebula is located. And he sees this nebula not as a tiny spot, but as an overwhelming cloud landscape. These clouds of cosmic dust, star clusters, and solar systems appear to be standing inalterably still. Yet they move faster than we can imagine. Here and there, one sees denser points and coalescences, which try to stand out individually in order to blossom momentarily, in the knowledge that: I am. And the friend stands in front of this landscape and wonders: "What is the difference here between what moves and what is moved?" And, astonished, he then turns back to the earth and thinks: "We are not exactly at the center of our own system. That may be why we view all events as something warped and unsatisfactory." Now one suddenly starts to speak and one does not stop until everything has been told.

But if it is a woman, then it can only be at midnight. It is very still in the house, as still as if there were no house around this room, in which there are two people. All that can be heard is the steady whispering of the narrator. This makes all solid things weightless, all boundaries are eliminated. He does not raise his voice as might be required by one passage or the other in his account. His hands make no explanatory gestures. He sits on the edge of her bed. They are both naked, but no longer heed it. Any agitated strangeness has disappeared from them. At first, she was startled to notice that his eyes were glued to her, but that he did not see her. Why is he telling me this, she wonders. Perhaps she does not understand everything because he expresses himself unclearly. Or perhaps she is not very interested; after all, what he is telling her is not very entertaining. But then she feels that his talking to her brings him closer to her than ever, and she yields to the joy of listening. And when he falters for an instant to light a cigarette, she quickly says: "Why don't you keep talking?" And then he keeps talking. Or else not, since it is no longer necessary.

You — I mean this being — had best ask me if you do not understand something. I know I am talking about things that have no validity now. I still have the words for them, I was part of it all, but they may no longer be quite apt. And there is much I will not talk about; I am not allowed, for it is too dangerous. One can think it and one can experience it. But if one uses words about it, then all existence becomes inauthentic.

At any rate, I went back to the city. I walked through the suburbs. The streets were as hushed as they used to be only in the two or three hours before daybreak, when life was still divided into yesterday and tomorrow. Indeed, they were even more hushed; for I cannot imagine that the breathing of hundreds of thousand of sleepers could not have made a sound. Except that in those days, no one stayed up to listen for it. And many people certainly talked in their sleep.

At first, I made an effort to tread loudly on the pavement. It was embarrassing to come so unnoticed and perhaps frighten someone. My lonesome steps ought to have aroused echoes from the empty building walls. But this did not happen. I was the only ear that heard me. It is not good to know that. It makes one very quiet.

It must have been around noon. The shops were open. In front of them stood baskets of food for sale and also carts that were about to be unloaded. And at each house door, a pail, a broom, and other things that did not use to be there at night. People had always been quite tidy about those things to avoid stumbling over them in the dark or simply out of fear of thieves. There were also toys lying around. A small yellow bear was leaning against a house wall, and next to it stood the small wooden wagon in which the bear had been brought here. The windows were open everywhere, laundry hung in front of some. But no smoke emerged from the chimneys.

Since the windows were open, it must have been summer. This occurs to me only now. I did not notice everything, I was too indifferent. Thus, I could not say whether there were flowers on the balconies. Indeed why not? But I did not perceive them as flowers. Earlier, by the same token, the trees on the streets of a city were perceived not as trees but as ornaments or as protection against sun and rain.

I entered various houses and mounted the stairs. I expected

nothing special, but I did it all the same. I would turn back on the second or third floor. Quite simply because it was not the right thing. I realized this because it was an effort to go up any further. Nothing smelled. No food, no unventilated clothing, no basement. There were no smells at all. Only *I* smelled — of rain and of myself.

Nor was it dark on the staircases or wherever it should have been dark. It is difficult talking about the colors. Nor am I reporting in sequence. There was no darkness and there was no light, it was simply clear. A boring clarity, which crept into everything. Perhaps places that should have been dark were merely somewhat less clear.

Earlier, when there used to be a moon, the situation was similar. One ought to picture the moonlight as five or ten times more intense. I do not even know if I am understood when I say "moon." That was something that had nothing of its own. To avoid being lost, it clung flatteringly to other things, absorbing color and character like a sponge and then acting as if it were all that itself. Something like that is worse than an enemy. It dazed everything with cold, blood-sucking light. The creatures utterly failed to notice that it was their own light that it had stolen from them. They thereby lost all reality.

Perhaps I am doing the moon an injustice. Oddly enough, most people felt more at home in the wan reflection of their being than in what they really were. Did they fear the light because it revealed their darkness? And what compelled them to deny their darkness? I keep asking myself that, although now it may make no sense to ponder it. It was their sickness.

However, there were things that retained their color and even increased in brilliance. Or so it seemed to me, because those were the only colors. The baskets in front of a produce store contained huge white cabbages as well as radishes or other pale roots. They looked very comfortable, spreading out so broadly that they were practically bloated with coziness. A bit further on, a store window and the street in front of it were virtually illuminated. The source was a group of big yellow cheeses on display there. But the most terrible part of it all was to pass the butcher shops; the pale meat of rows of slaughtered animals hanging in the stores appeared to be the only living thing.

There is no need to talk about those disgusting things; one might just as well forget them. Yes, I would rather assume that I was mistaken; after what happened, and given the situation I was in, how could I claim to have an accurate sense of judgment? Perhaps I was still thinking in yesterday's familiar terms and not in terms that were adequate to the present state of things. But later on, in a different part of the city, I saw something that I cannot forget and will not forget. It was in the window of a jewelry shop. I mean the pearls. For gold and polished stones, any of the things that can gleam and glitter in light, were outshone by those pearls. I do not feel I am mistaken: they were living and breathing. They must have been enormously valuable; but I had been no connoisseur even earlier. Except that it is important that they now caught my eye and that I do not care to forget them. Gray and milky pearls. But that says nothing. Their gray had a memory of all the colors that no longer existed. What a delicate refuge! Or an inkling of all colors as they are to be born some day. I stood in front of the shop for a long time, I could not tear myself away. I am still standing in front of it mentally. I should have taken some of the pearls along to give them as presents. For if it is a woman to whom I am telling this, I believe that any woman, tomorrow and always, would be delighted. Who could have prohibited me from simply taking the pearls? After all, everything was mine. But it never even occurred to me.

The only shop I entered was a bakery. There was a bell on the door. I waited for quite some time; such is upbringing. Then I took a roll from the counter and left. For a while, the bell shrieked and yelled after me; it was happy to be heard by someone. The roll was fresh, I ate it on the way. Not because I was hungry. Granted, I must have been hungry; but I ate in order to have something between my teeth and not to get lost.

I knew precisely: there was no chance of my encountering anyone. Not even a dog. Nor was I scared of that. But now, looking back, I wonder what might have happened if I *had* met someone. Can there be any doubt? If it had been a human being, I would have killed him on the spot. I am not very brave, nor very strong or skillful. I have always cravenly avoided fistfights and have never killed anyone. Or have I? I now recall that I occasionally had to dream that something was lying in the cellar or buried under a bush in the garden, not very deep — no, not under a bush, but under a heap of moldering, slippery boards piled up along a wall: a corpse. It haunted me, and I lived in unrelenting fear that it might be found. At one point, they must have discovered it, for I was to be executed. It was on the outskirts of the city, in the midst of allotment gardens. Several well-dressed gentlemen were present. Not too far away, the suburban houses stood like a wall. In a beseeching voice, I informed the prosecutor of what I had already accomplished. I cannot say what I meant. And I informed him of what I would still accomplish. What a ludicrous scene! What a wretched lack of pride! I can still see him shrugging and my defense attorney glancing at me and imper-

ceptibly shaking his head. What I felt at this slight movement
is not to be described. Ah, to think that one cannot say precisely: I did not do this or that. For perhaps I *did* do it after all,
but simply failed to realize it. Yet it is suddenly obvious that
one is by no means the person who always lived according to
everyone else's customs and took pains to behave no differently from what was demanded of him. Then the whole sham
collapses, and one stands there with nothing to hold on to. But
that would take us too far afield. If I keep talking about this,
then even the name of the corpse will come to my lips. That
would be dreadful.

I was saying that had I encountered anyone, I would have
killed him on the spot. That goes without saying. Incidentally,
it would have been a merciful deed; no one could have
endured even a moment of this state of total freedom without
going mad. Can a madman still be called human? However, I
am not claiming that I would have acted out of mercy. Indeed,
as soon as I had noticed him, I would have hidden behind a
corbeling and then pounced on him.

If it had been a human being! It could also have been
merely a hallucination, and I had to convince myself of that
as fast as possible. And he — I mean if he had been a human
being, then he could only have been one like me. And this
person might have been swifter and stronger than I. In any
case, he would have made the very same effort to get rid of
me on the spot. As it was, there could be no one else. That
would have meant that the end had not yet come, and each
of us would have been obligated to bring about the end no
matter what.

One is seized with immeasurable woe. We must avoid
thinking about it. Ever since I became aware of myself, I have

been seeking this other. And he me. In order to speak to him as I now speak. To give each other names in which all the conflict in the world could be forgotten forever. Where was he? For he was here. His image *was* inside me, therefore his being had to be somewhere outside me. And I frequently spoke his name. And I sometimes heard the name he gave me. Did we pass one another? Were we blind and hardened by the futilities of the days that hatefully surrounded us? And now, with these hands, which wanted to do good to one another, we would have strangled each other, because it was too late.

We must avoid talking about it. I have done so only because I no longer have a name that says anything about me, and because nothing gives me a name that compels me to imagine anything. But you are to know what I am.

However, I did not meet that other. I was all alone and I walked through the large, empty city. I do not know how long or what gave me the strength. I do not believe I could do it a second time. Have I not said: There are things that are more easily done than thought. Thus I came to the center of the city and to large squares that were surrounded by gigantic buildings. Earlier, the country had been governed from here. One can walk past them and forget them; there is nothing real to be found in them except for the anxious efforts that people have always made to capture all reality in laws. They do not say: If you are distressed, come to me! They say: You are not to feel distressed! From proud galleries, they proclaimed to the populace what it wanted to hear: that everything was in order. And next door there was a theater, where people actually watched performances of their destiny such as they never dared to live it. All this is very bizarre.

Finally, I stepped into a home. It was a not very large one-family house, which stood in a garden. I entered the house because it happened to be in my way. Or because the garden gate and the front door were open. Or also only because I was fed up with running around and it was time to put an end to it. One should not assume that there is more to it. In hindsight, of course, it would seem as if this house had been my goal and had been expecting me. But that is not true. I had no goal. I could just as easily have entered any of the thousand other homes; after all, everything was mine, and I do not know what I would have encountered there.

You see, this house was awaiting guests, although not me. I made a point of wiping my shoes on the mat in order to avoid dirtying the polished floors. But I would have left no traces anyhow. I walked down a hallway, various doors stood ajar, but I went past them without peering inside. I headed straight for the kitchen, which was located in the back of the house. I have no idea why I did that; even now, it makes no sense. Perhaps I felt that I was not appropriately dressed to enter the front rooms as a visitor. But all that is unimportant.

Pots stood on the stove. They looked as if they had only just been cooking something. Naturally, no fire was burning. I raised a lid, it was not hot. Yet I did not have the impression that the food had cooled off. No, the fat had not coagulated. I did not notice whether steam was emerging from the pots. Nor did I try any of the food. Most likely nothing would have had a taste. They must have been about to carry the food to the table. The meal could begin. Everything was clean and unspoiled. After all, there were no flies.

And that was good. For a fly would have probably been unendurable. Imagine that the persons with whom you always lived together and most closely have suddenly left you.

And now you are standing in what used to be the household kitchen. And all the indifferent objects that were heedlessly employed day in, day out, and that were so modest as not to intrude, even though they were somehow necessary — should not they too have shared our destiny? A lid no longer quite fits a pot because it is twisted, or the front of a spoon is worn smooth from so much stirring. But we no longer notice such things, we are used to them; after all, these minor defects developed through our living together — yes, and all these objects are still here, and you do not know why. A fly only has to buzz, and you are done for.

Eventually, I did go to the front of the house after all, looking for the dining room. It was next to the front door. The table was set for twelve people, I instantly counted. It looked very festive: the white tablecloth, the settings, crystal decanters of wine, and silver candelabras. There may have been flowers too, I cannot picture it otherwise. I gazed at everything, I even touched a few objects. I believe that I actually shifted and rearranged one thing or another. To test it, I sat down at the table. There was a seat at the narrow end, opposite the open glass doors, which led to a terrace. Another setting was at my right. No one came to serve me, no invisible hands placed food in front of me. Nor, incidentally, did I expect it. Then I stood up again and gingerly pushed the chair back to the table. A painting hanging on the wall had caught my eye. A bleak landscape with water. Or, more precisely: no landscape, but something that had been or was yet to become a landscape. The colors reminded me of the pearls. That is very bizarre. The person who had painted the picture and those who had hung it in their room in order to view it constantly must have known a great deal more than their daily existence seemed to prove. Where was the defect?

The next room had books, two walls full. These people must have been well-read. A small piano stood there, it was open, and a score was on the music desk. Why should I describe all this? It was like everywhere else, a bit more tasteful perhaps; but that was not it. Something was missing; above all, it was not what I was looking for. But just what *was* I looking for? I wandered, through the streets of the city and through these rooms. What had prompted me to return to the city in the first place? I certainly could not assume that it still existed. And I had even less reason to think that it would release me again, and that I would now be standing in the rain on this high, treeless plateau, amid nameless, exhausted sleepers — whom one, likewise nameless, does not dare call human beings — in order to talk about it. For none of this happened to supply me with an interesting story to tell. But somebody has to speak about it. It could be that something unexpectedly pops up among the words, something that should not be forgotten; and once it is articulated, it begins to live. Sometimes it seems to me — but perhaps I am wrong, and it need not be taken all too seriously — that I returned to the city because of those colors. I mean the colors of the pearls and of the painting.

I stood at the mirror for a long time. Or did I sit in front of it? Here, my story gets confused because I was very tired. Ask me if you want any details. Being a man, I do not notice everything. It may be that I overlook precisely the most important things.

The mirror was like a narrow gate, I could have passed through it comfortably.

Yes, it was a woman's room. One must bear in mind that the rooms and the objects no longer gave off any kind of smell. That was why I did not perceive it right away. But all sorts of objects that should have made me aware of it must have been lying about. Gloves or stockings or a handkerchief. I now remember that some face powder was strewn on the glass shelf of one of the small cabinets next to the mirror. I traced a sinuous line in the powder with my finger, but since it looked like an *S*, I quickly blew it away; otherwise, some unknown person whose name happened to start with that letter might think that somebody was calling him and trying to cast a spell on him. I should probably have looked for a comb; there must have been one lying there. But who thinks of such a thing? I could then say whether the woman who lived in that room was young or old, blonde or dark. Yet if I think about it: why should, of all things, a woman's combed-out hair have preserved its color and character? It would have probably looked like a cold spider web. But those are secrets that I do not have to know.

I believe that she was blond. I am thinking of the small, delicate canary feather that was inserted as a bookmark into a notebook. The notebook was lying on her small vanity table. It was so close to the outer edge that it was bound to fall any moment. Opening the page that was marked by the feather, I read:

> What I so often fear in deepest sleep
> Is that we might throw caution to the winds,
> Oh, pleasure sweet, that lures and tortures me;
> To die too soon, most terrible of thoughts.
>
> It could come in the midst of conversation
> Or outdoors, in the street: we could collapse
> If suddenly we met each other....

Is that not strange? I do not mean that people wrote such verses and printed and read them. That too is strange, but I have already talked about it. I mean that to judge by these verses, the woman would have had to be dark. But perhaps that is only a male conjecture, and if another woman heard those verses, she would secretly make fun of them.

I stood at her mirror and peered into it. There, I saw everything that was behind me and everything that surrounded me. But before me there was nothing, and I too was not in there. A human being would have cried out in shock: I am lost.

I am thinking of a small lake high in the mountains over the border of existence, where things have always been the way they now are everywhere. The gentle deer avoided drinking from the lake, and the paths of the hunters did not lead there. The encircling peaks that were supposed to guard it acted as if it were not there and they gazed outward. Even their shadows paled and leaned away from the shores of the lake; for a different darkness flowed from its depth, striking everything dumb. In the valley, people said that the angels were afraid to fly across this lake because their reflections would be lost in it. And that once a star, weary of being only a star, had plunged from heaven to earth and sunk into the lake. That is a fairy tale. Such eyes existed too.

Do you think I am dead? Oh well, that is a stupid question. And if you to whom I am speaking are a friend, then it is also a superfluous question. For it then makes little difference whether we are alive or dead; all that is important is that we speak with one another. But if you are a woman, then I can feel your hair at any time or graze your breasts with astonished fingers, and it will be obvious that I am alive. They used to tell us that the dead sometimes return, but they always knew that they had died, and they did not try to deceive anyone. On the contrary: they instantly warned us not to touch them, and, with a quiet gesture, they asked us to forgive the intrusion caused by their unseemly coming. They came only because they had missed something or because they were unable to part with a habit. Ah, it reminds me of the old pharmacist who had previously lived in my home. The room where I now had my bed used to be his dining room. He would come every night and go over to his sideboard to pour himself a jigger of his home-made schnapps. He made sure not to disturb me by, say, bumping into the rearranged furniture. But no matter how quiet he was and no matter how considerate, he could not prevent the floorboards from creaking slightly, and so I did notice him all the same. Later on, he gave up coming; apparently, it was no longer necessary.

But as regards myself: If I was dead, why was I alone in the city? Where were the other countless dead who had died with me? Not to mention those who had died at some earlier point? What a teeming! No, I could not be dead. For only a living person could be as lonesome as I was. Earlier, I had had far more reason to ask myself whether I was really alive when I compared myself with others. Or when I read in a book that a healthy man had to live such and such a life style. Often I was disconcerted by the people in the street. They scrutinized me differently from the way they sized up any other passerby. If it was a man, they would check to see whether they could compete with him. And if it was a woman or a girl, to see whether she was lovable. Or merely to avoid running into the person coming towards them. But when I walked by, it was different. They stopped short as if I had not been there a moment earlier and had stepped out of a cloud right in front of them. And once I was past, then I had instantly vanished as far as they were concerned, and they believed they had been mistaken and gave it no further thought. It was very unpleasant for me to startle them; that was why I preferred crossing the street, if I could do so in time. But I could not always avoid meeting them. Even when I was with good friends and left them, I would reproach myself for abandoning them — indeed, already reproach myself on the stairs right after the front door locked behind me. They may still be sitting together and thinking: Why, he was just sitting with us. Why did he not leave us anything? It is as if he had not been here. Or vice versa — and this is even more serious — they feel as if they themselves had suddenly died and were already forgotten by me. Nor would it have helped any if I had returned and told them quite heartily that they were wrong and that I was more earnestly trying to see things from their side than they from mine. They would only have gaped at me in astonishment and doubted my sanity.

At that time, in front of the mirror, I did not doubt for an instant that I was alive. It was not I that was dead; it could only be that the mirror had died. I also examined it to find out. I wanted to push it away from the wall to check behind it, but I was unable to do so.

The other possibility did not occur to me — I mean that my image could have perished. And how could I have thought of it? We cannot imagine any person without his reflection, and it is questionable whether a living creature without a reflection can even be described as human. If, for example, the sky cannot be reflected in my eyes, is it then still the sky? But if not, then what is it? Perhaps something similar, but in no case that which used to be called the sky. I also believe that I occasionally noticed that whenever a flower is admired for its beauty, it really blossoms, becoming even more beautiful, until we ourselves blush, and there is no saying which of the two has been gifted. People used to think that they knew this very precisely; and now?

I had also not noticed back then that I had likewise lost my name. After all, I had no opportunity to determine this. There was no one to call me or address me, and I for my part never addressed myself by the name that others used when they wanted something from me. And I had even less reason for knowing that I owed my life purely to the fact that I had been connected so loosely with my name and my image that they could not pull me along when they perished. It was simply like a banknote that slips from your pocket unnoticed, that is all. The wind wafts it away; someone may find it and know what to do with it; or it may fall into a puddle and dissolve.

I was not so much terrified by all this as astonished. Eventually, I grew tired of thinking and I got into the bed. Yes, there was a bed in the room. I simply uncovered it, pushing aside the nightshirt underneath the blanket, and I lay down just as I was, soaked with rain and splattered with mud.

I fell asleep instantly and dreamed....

The window curtain bellied into the room with a soft breath. A bumblebee buzzed into the room, flew against the wall several times, and then found its way out again. In the garden, two children were playing under the window. One of them shouted: We have to go home. From the street came the steps of passersby and disjointed sounds of their conversation. A bit further off, a trolley jingled, and the conductor blew the departure whistle. Then the street grew noisier and noisier. Cars roared by, howled warnings at the street corners.

Somewhere freight trains rolled across a bridge. In the harbor, a steamer putting out to sea emitted three dull moans, and a tugboat responded, shrill and agitated. Eventually, the noise became so loud that one could no longer hear it all.

It was a late afternoon towards the end of June. It must have been a fairly warm day, but the room was now on the shady side. The green reflection of a sunny lawn clung to the ceiling. Somewhere, the lindens were blossoming; the sweet fragrance threatened to give me a headache. Three yellow roses stood on a small, round mahogany table. I picked up the vase to smell the roses, but then replaced it, unsatisfied. As I did so, two petals dropped off from a rose and then lay on the shiny table top like ships on a windless sea. I tried not to make a sound. Irresolute, I paced up and down the carpet, listening for life in the house.

Suddenly, the doorbell rang, and I recoiled. Then someone emerged from the kitchen (I could tell by the kitchen noises reaching my ear), walked through the hall, and opened the front door. Some words were exchanged, then another door was opened, a loud tangle of voices emerged, and then the house was quiet again. The person who had opened the front door returned to the kitchen. I had been afraid that he would knock on my door or even come in; but he did not do so.

After a while, I pulled myself together, left the room, and stole along the hall runner to the front of the house. The hall smelled of frying. Actually, I was planning to leave the house unnoticed; but I inadvertently clutched the knob of the door to the room from which the voices were coming. The knob was pleasantly cool, it dispelled all my qualms. I opened the door and stepped inside.

All eyes turned towards me. The conversation faltered for an endless second. Then I was loudly greeted. They had been expecting me, which did not surprise me in the least. I *am* recounting a dream, mind you. One of the people promptly caught my eye. He called to me: "A distinguished gentleman is always the last to come." It was his intonation that made me prick up my ears. You must pay very close attention to him, I told myself, otherwise he will notice something. As I soon found out, he was considered my friend. He kept addressing me as "My friend." It was very irksome having such a watchdog next to me.

And it was he who made me aware of the lady of the house. It was not his words but his observant eyes that made me realize there was something special about her. You see, I was not the host. Coming towards me, she said … No, I do not think she said it; she shook my hand, and I knew that she wanted to say: "I was starting to think you would not come." This was not meant as a reproach, but it instantly made me very sad because I could not help her. I smiled embarrassedly in her direction. I avoided speaking to her and looking at her. Nor are such things necessary if one wishes to get to know a person. On the contrary, they are often merely distracting.

It is foolish of me to talk about it. But I assume you would like to know who she was and what she looked like and what sort of dress she was wearing. I would tell you if I could; I would certainly not keep it to myself. Nor would I be doing her an injustice by talking about her to a friend or another woman. And why should I not have had something to do with a woman back then? Besides, one can know a man properly only by knowing how he feels about women. Without them, he is not quite tangible, and he fades away like a word that is shouted into emptiness. In short, it was, of course, the woman in whose bed I was sleeping, but there is not much more I can say about her. She was there and was present. And I was most likely dreaming and was not present. Yes, that was probably how it was. Perhaps I will succeed nevertheless in describing some small gesture to recognize her by.

When I say I was dreaming, I am not making a value judgment. People always used to warn us about dreams. They claimed: Dreams are but shadows, and only reality has substance. As if a dream that we dream has no reality. Indeed, the opposite could have been easily proved in their language. For when I awake in the morning and, because of my nightly experience, I am a different person than on the previous evening (indeed, I behave differently than I would like to; I drop an agreed-on plan or make objections, thereby inducing the people who deal with me to change their attitude towards me and behave differently), how can a dream that has such effects have no reality? How much did people even know about this reality anyway? One afternoon, when I was working in a bank, a clerk next to me abruptly sighed: "Ah, and this morning I was in such a good mood." Yet, demonstrably, nothing unpleasant had happened to him that day — at least, nothing that he himself or we others could view as a reason for his mood swing. Had there been a shift in the air pressure? The people would have preferred that explanation, but they knew quite well that it explained nothing. They were afraid of something they could not account for, and they tried to cover up this insecurity with loud proverbs. It would have been better if they had not felt so secure.

All I am saying is that for the reality of that woman, it makes no difference whether I was dreaming or waking. Incidentally, I was not married to her.

I have probably neglected to mention that there could not

have been anything striking about my clothes. They were exactly what was expected of me, and I paid them no further heed. People spoke to me, and I said yes or no, as they wished, I nodded, smiled, or listened with an earnest face. It was not the least bit difficult. For instance, one of them took me into a corner and talked away at me. He proposed some joint business venture or something of the kind. I replied: Yes, that is something we can talk about, or: Let me sleep on it. And he left me contentedly.

We were all young or, more precisely, none of us was old. Ridiculous as it sounds: it was as if we were children pretending to be grownups. We would have been more genuine had we played with dolls somewhere or played hide-and-seek, or spun tops in the street. Instead, we had gotten it into our heads to play adults, and we took the roles very seriously. To appear believable, we exaggerated what looked typical in adult behavior: say, the bows, the conduct at meals, the idioms, and what not. We had even adopted some bizarre crotchets that had struck us in an uncle or an aunt. I sense that we even played at love, because we felt it was required. Naturally, I cannot claim this with any certainty, but I suspect that a few of them thought they loved each other and probably embraced and slept together at night, because they knew that that was what grownups did. It must have been a very dangerous game; because, by playing at things for which they lacked the maturity — even though, perhaps much to their own amazement, they found the necessary skill within themselves — they stunted their own growth. In fact, people generally talked too much about love, and since they therefore made it too easy for themselves, few of them really achieved it; which always provoked great sighs.

Was I the eldest? Am I really that old? I look at the sleepers around me, they could have been lying here for an eternity because no shepherd awoke them. I am the only one standing erect among them. If there are any eyes left in the void, they could use me as a guidepost. But I stare into the wet gray, and there is nothing I can measure by. It can be a beginning or an end. How am I to decide? It would make no sense talking of near and far.

Naturally, I know that there is something lying behind me, but it can no longer be proved. To be credible, I would have to produce remnants or shards; but there is nothing left. Only words, and words too are no longer valid. For what does it mean to say: there is something behind me. Earlier, there used to be nothing more reliable than chronology. Everything was precisely divided and could be expressed in numbers. One man was thirty years old, and another had lived a thousand years ago. The calculation was correct, no doubt, but the premise is no longer the same. Time is shattered. How can there be a yesterday? How can there be a thousand years ago? All I have to do is turn to the people who lived a thousand years ago, and I can converse with them. So what good are the numbers? For if I do not turn to those people, then they do not exist, and no number alters the situation in the least. And it is the same with you, my friend, to whom I am speaking; you exist because you are listening to me. Or am I like a newborn baby, who claims: I am already nine months old. And a lot older, since I already lived in the blood of my parents and forebears. Yes, I have been living from the very beginning. That would probably be a childish statement, and yet ...?

If ever it should again become necessary to articulate things in numbers, because otherwise people would get lost, then I will begin not with yesterday, not with my walk through the city, not with my dream; instead, we will have to reckon: so and so many hours or days or years from the moment when I was able to speak about it.

At the table, I sat next to the hostess. It was the very place that I had tried out previously, when I was alone. This happened as a matter of course, and no one objected. We were celebrating something, and the hostess was the celebrant, and so was I, since I was sitting next to her. I do not know what was being celebrated. In any case, we wanted to be happy.

If only I knew her name. And my friend's name, yes, his especially; for he was basically not what I picture as a friend. In no case was he like the friend to whom I may now be speaking. I could make up names, and everything would be fine. For example, the name Lysander would fit my friend quite nicely, I do not know why. Lysander was a general, who won a few important battles. He must have been a highly capable man, but I never met him in person. Yet who knows — I may run into him eventually. Or he may come to me on his own and take me to task when he learns that I have given his name to someone else. And what great disorder might result from that. That is why I would rather let it be.

And "hostess" — what does that mean anyway? "Friend" would be better. She receives the guest; in her home, he can cleanse himself of the grime of his wanderings, she gives him new clothes, something to eat, and a place to sleep. And when the time comes, she sends him on his way with many gifts. That used to be the custom. She most likely also gave him good advice for his journey, and it was certainly not her fault if the guest did not leave her as a wiser man. Her name — I mean the hostess, next to whom I was allowed to sit — is

probably something like Iona. Perhaps a letter is missing. I
know of no woman who had this name. Perhaps it is not so
significant for women. The sound is more important. They
wrap themselves in it, and if the color is becoming, they keep
the name. Iona evokes a hilly land by the sea. There is a surf
and there are also lonely desert islands. The landscape is often
foggy, and if the sun ever shines, it is magical.

At dinner, she must have assumed that I knew her name.
We were sitting very close together. I sensed her warmth and
thereby also sensed her question: Why are you acting like
that? For though I made every effort to conceal it, she must
have sensed my question: Just who are you? So the two of us,
while participating in the general conversation, listened
closely to whatever was behind the words.

Sometimes our hands touched. I do not know what her hands
were like. As for mine ... Well, you can see them for yourself. On
her left hand, she wore an old silver ring with an opal. I wasted
a great deal of effort trying to find out whether the ring was a
present from me. When could I have given it to her anyway?

I thought of a wooden arbor standing in the garden of a
tenant farm. The arbor contained a real room, which, incidentally, I never entered. In front of it there was a small open
terrace with a table and benches surrounded by grape leaves.
Antlers and a few painted targets hung on the solid wall of the
terrace. One of the targets showed a mountain cock court-
ing precariously on a pine tree. The other picture showed a
stag with a tremendous vapor issuing from its mouth. The
most exciting picture showed a struggle between a forester
and a poacher high in the mountains. The poacher was
kneeling behind a boulder; naturally, he had a black beard
while the forester was respectably clean-shaven. The poacher

was also wearing an open, tattered shirt and buckskin trousers. Next to him lay a chamois kid; yes, a kid. The fiend had shot it in the chest region; to make this quite clear, the artist had not spared the red paint. However, it was not yet decided who would win this hunting-rifle duel.

The arbor stood virtually concealed in the blaze of noon. The low main house was visible through the grape vines. Wherever the wall was not camouflaged by espalier fruit, its harsh yellow-white hurt the eyes. The twigs of the currant bushes, full of red clusters, hung over the fence of the nearby vegetable garden. At first, the clattering of plates and dishes could be heard from the kitchen. But by now, everyone must have been asleep, like the yellow hound in the open front door. Or else, the farm hands, male and female, were out in the fields. The hush was occasionally broken only by the drowsy crooning and clucking of a hen. It was the hour of day that so closely resembles midnight; although one can see everything, it all blurs insensibly into light and heat, just as, in the darkness of night, things lose their familiar stance.

The cloth covering the table on the arbor terrace had an old-fashioned blue cross-stitch pattern. A vase containing bell flowers stood on it. And two young people, almost children, were sitting there. The boy was reading poetry aloud, and the girl had folded her hands in the lap of her white dress and was listening attentively. You must not laugh. When I see that picture, sentimental words come to my lips, such as: Happiness! And youth! And fullness! And yet it is nonsense! Where would I have taken the money back then to give the girl such a valuable ring, which a priest must have worn in ancient times.

Turning away, I walk across the crowded square of a metropolis. I do not consider it impossible that this is the same city to which I then returned later on. It is a filthy winter morning, but I do not notice it, for it fits me so nicely. Very many cars drive past, preventing me from crossing the street. So for a while, together with other people, I have to wait by a monument in the middle of the square. A green man sits there on a ruddy marble pedestal. He clutches a scroll. His hand is half covered with a lace cuff that falls out of his sleeve. He has a braid. But his forehead and his shoulders are soiled with white stripes by the sparrows. At last, I can hurry across the roadway and I charge straight towards a mailbox. Then, something occurs to me, and I reach into my left coat pocket.

You see, early in the morning, I took a girl to an ocean liner. So the story I am narrating must have happened in a port. Perhaps she was no longer a girl, I do not know. I accompanied her to customs, they had checked her papers and opened the valise that I was carrying for her. The burgundy taffeta silk dress that she had worn on the previous evening lay on top. We had been with the people she was living with. I believe we also danced. After we were done with customs, we stood on the swaying pontoon, waiting for the harbor ferry, which was supposed to take us to the other side. Dock workers were sailing with us. We did not say a word. It was damp and hazy. We were freezing. The ferry crushed and ground the white ice floes. On the opposite shore, we had to walk for a time amid bleak warehouses and across the desolate pavement of the docks until we found the steamer. I gave her the valise, and we shook hands. We did not embrace, no. Then she went up the gangway. How tiny she looked against the high wall of the ship. And I too stood down below, small and lost. She glanced back a few times. On deck, she was greeted by a crewman. That was the last I saw of her. I returned home without a thought in my mind. At the letter box, I remembered that she had given me a postcard to mail. I pulled it out and read: "Dear Grandmother, On my last day at home ..." I read no further. I quickly thrust the card into the letter box. The lid slammed shut. I had to control myself to keep from bursting into tears. So many people were passing back and forth, all of them had something to do and somewhere to go. Why had this girl left her homeland? Hold on, I know. She did not care to wait.

But she sailed very far away, and the woman sitting next to me could never have worn a burgundy frock.

And again my eyes alight on the opal. It is the dead of night. A man stands at the second-story window of a cheap house. He stands in the dark. He can be seen only when the night wind pushes the foliage of the trees slightly aside, so that the moonlight falls upon his figure. He thinks: "Yes, I want to suggest it to her." But it is already too late for the suggestion; he should have come with it an hour earlier. At that time, two people, like thousands of other pairs of lovers in the same city, stood leaning in the shade of a house, and the world around them was an indifferent hubbub. Across the street, a construction site was fenced off with raw planks. A circus had glued its posters on the boards. There, in the glow of the street light, one could see a number of elephants involved in all sorts of mischief; each elephant's trunk held on to the next one's little tail.

That was when he should have made the suggestion to her that he was now pondering: "Why do we not die together? For there is nothing beyond this but death."

Yet her hands were much too hard for such a heavy ring to suit her.

Suddenly, I forgot all that. Without a sound of lament, the hostess at my side vanished from my thoughts.

At the other end of the table, a conversation had begun, forcing me to concentrate my entire being on it. They were discussing an event that had occurred at noon and was on everyone's mind. I too was familiar with it.

At precisely twelve noon, two huge, unknown birds from the west had appeared above the city. Flying slowly, almost without moving their wings, and at not too high an altitude, they floated, seeking, across the houses, circled the tower of the city hall three times, and then vanished in the direction from which they had come. When it was over, people exchanged uncertain glances, wondering if they had fallen prey to a hallucination; and ever since, they had been talking and arguing about nothing else. Indeed, there were no two consistent statements about the event. The dimensions ascribed to the birds were nonsensical; their color was now white, now black; and extremely clever people maintained that the tops of the wings were white and the bottoms black. It was not even certain how long the whole incident had lasted. Everyone claimed to have held his breath for an eternity; but in reality, clocks had barely advanced. When they calculated it afterwards, not even a single minute was missing — either in the daily schedules of individual people or in the timetables of public transportation.

As I have said, I too had seen the birds. I was standing at the staircase window in a large office building. It may also have been a government building or a bank. Incidentally, I must have had a steady job in this edifice, for I recall that I often stood at this window. It gave onto a canal and bridges, and the green tower of the city hall was visible in the background. In summertime, the canal was crowded with barges and tugboats; in cold winters, its entangled ice floes made it look like a glacier landscape. On a chain that was drawn straight across the canal in order to hold the lantern, gulls perched like a string of pearls, restlessly gaping around to see if any food had been thrown out for them. Then, all at once, they shrieked as they left their perches, gliding off and disappearing. The water in the canal was usually dirty and unpleasant; the houses directly lining it were of ugly red bricks. This made the color of the water even uglier. But sometimes, in spring and autumn, the water reflected the green of the city hall tower together with the soft azure sky, and then everything was virtually enchanted.

The stairwell was always crowded. Apprentices dashed down the steps, taking several at a time. Visitors arrived, others said goodbye, and something was called out to them over the banisters. Employees emerged from the offices to grab a smoke in the halls or exchange a few words with a girl. But suddenly, it was all gone. One felt all alone in the world.

I watched the birds and had the impression that they were looking for me. Perhaps, incidentally, everyone else thought the same about themselves. Curious, neither stirring nor hiding, I waited to see if they would find me. When they were gone, I almost regretted that I had not cried out: Here I am! There was an indescribable hush during that timeless pause. Wherever one of these birds cast its shadow, all life cringed. Now, afterwards, I know that it was as hushed as I so painfully felt it later on, during my lonesome walk through the city. Naturally, there were many people who had not seen the birds because they were occupied in closed rooms. But strikingly enough, they too had the impression that something extraordinary had happened, and that they, as they stated afterwards, had not dared to move for an endlessly long time. We noticed the same thing about the dogs, and some people claimed that the heads of the flowers had drooped, only to perk up again right away. This alone must have been very terrifying.

No sooner was it over than an enormous chattering rose in the city. I myself spoke to nobody, I quite deliberately avoided it. Something of the hush of that moment was still around me, so that I could not be reached by questions or even by the looks of the bewildered people. I stepped outdoors immediately and, without even reflecting, I headed in the direction of the birds, towards the unknown. I do not mean to boast, I am only saying that it was not an escape.

Now, I probably look like a miserable refugee. I have no name and no mirror image. I find it impossible to state what I used to be considered among people. I am in no way distinguished from the ones lying around me. I have scrutinized their faces to glean what has preserved them from the fate of other human beings. I would like to get to know the law governing us all. But their faces are utterly blank, they seem to have no past. One can look through their eyes, there is nothing to hold on to. Yes, the wind blows through; behind them lies the same bleak immensity as in front of them.

As for me, I can only say this much: Whatever that past may have been, I left it like a prison. I had to control myself in the streets to keep from jubilantly shouting: At last! Although I knew that now the hardest part was beginning.

However, I want to return to my dream. At the table, they were talking about that event. They were surprised that no one had had enough presence of mind to photograph the birds. Or shoot them down. Or have them pursued in airplanes. They railed against the government that permitted such a thing, and they were amazed that something like this could have happened in the first place. Yet uncertainty was blatant in everything they said. Even if a person uttered something that was meant to be superior and sarcastic, it was more of a concealed question, and many glasses of wine were drunk, virtually to wash down a bad taste. Finally, someone put an end to the whole thing by asking: "What do the evening papers say?"

In the past, people did not rely on their own judgment. They had suitable people who were supposed to report on everything and express an opinion that seemed the most appropriate for the majority. In the evening, one could read it punctually, and then, if one spoke to a neighbor before going to bed, one discovered that he was of the same mind. Thus everything was in order, and worrisome enigmas could not emerge.

I know that this handful of people who have been driven together here by chance are waiting only for someone to tell them what to think. Perhaps that is the only reason why they are sleeping so long, although I must admit that it can also be due to exhaustion and hunger. I also believe that they are already counting on my being the one to come up with an opinion for them. I found this out before returning to the city. There was a man whom I thought younger and livelier than the others. I leaned over him and asked him something. Perhaps I asked him whether he wanted to accompany me. I virtually blew into the ashes, surmising that there was a spark left underneath. It would be more agreeable if I knew of someone who could stand at my side. But it was no use badgering him. He was not accustomed to being questioned. Yes, I now recall what I asked him: Did he think that the city and everything else were still the same as before, and that it might be we who had changed? Indeed, to be perfectly clear, I also asked him whether he believed that we were dead. But he did not understand me. There was only a touch of poignant willingness in his tired face — willingness to receive something from me, an order, an idea, but absolutely no question. If I had told him: We are dead! he would have been satisfied. He addressed me in the polite form, while I used the familiar.

Shall I now make up something that they can believe in? And why? I myself do not need these people. After walking alone through the city and returning, I know that I can live quite well on a depopulated earth without dying of loneliness. I will live with my words, with the ones I have left. Some of them may perhaps take root, and this will give them a certain power over me, to which I must acquiesce. That is not so bad; it is a law to which I gladly submit. But these people around me will, at most, disturb me in the process; for I will have power over them, and heaven help me if I refrain from exercising it. They would kill me. Nothing makes people more unfree than having power, and only slaves love being powerful.

If only I knew what has saved these people. If I could only fathom chance. Could these people be words that I once uttered heedlessly and that have become flesh? Professor So-and-so, a well-known zoologist, stated that there was nothing extraordinary about the possibility that, under certain conditions — in this case, obviously in Arctic regions — familiar animals could develop to unusual sizes. The two birds, he said, undoubtedly belonged to the class of seagulls. An expedition was already being fitted out to explore their breeding grounds and everything else. A report would be issued shortly.

Incidentally, he went on, there was no cause for anxiety.

So much for the newspapers. The man who kept addressing me as "My Friend" had not yet joined the conversation: he seemed entirely absorbed in pouring salt on a red-wine stain in the white tablecloth. But now he suddenly began: "What do we care about the blabber in the newspapers, since we are fortunate enough to have someone here who knows more about it. Let us ask him. Maybe he will do us the favor of replying." He looked at me, and all other eyes likewise turned towards me.

I could feel myself blanch. I did not dare stir. I did not even dare to think; for I felt as if he could read my mind and was therefore scoffing at me. He was far more intelligent than I am; I had often admired his mind and been ashamed of my own ignorance. Yet I felt odd about him; he never really said anything that struck me as new. In general, he only said things that I felt had already occurred to me, except that I did not voice them or that I was not endowed with the ability to voice them. Upon hearing them from him, I grabbed my head and thought: Yes, of course, that is it. At the same time, I had a sense of regret that these ideas had been uttered, and the spoken thoughts detached themselves from me and became alien to me and hostile.

Thus, when he addressed me now, his words were like my own thought, which I had not permitted to be uttered. I suddenly realized that I must know more about the afternoon event than the others. But was it not too early to talk about it? Was not this "friend" of mine trying to pull an unripe fruit from the branch?

For I swear to you, my true friend, you who are listening to this, or I swear to you, the woman so patiently lying next to me in bed, that I did not know it at the time. In any case, did not know it enough to have words for it. And what do I really know about it now? Not much more than the external facts, and I even saw very little of them; there were things I did not understand and much that I have forgotten.

And what if I *had* known it? How should I have behaved? If, for instance, one happens to know that a good friend's favorite child is to die within a week, and the father now comes and makes plans for his child's future and would like to discuss them with somebody, what should one say to him? For example: Save your energy, it is useless? Or one has learned — and one is the only one — that the Deluge will burst in tomorrow. There is absolutely no salvation, except for one person, and that one person is oneself. Oh, what a burden for that person to live from today until tomorrow! If he endures this, he is truly afflicted. If he were to tell people, then — assuming that they believed it, which is not probable — the sole consequence would be that the Deluge would already begin today. So one has to keep silent, although that is the hardest thing to do.

Let us not forget that I am recounting a dream; for during the time that we could have been sitting at the table, I was entirely somewhere else. I was standing on the threshold of my room. Thus, contrary to my original goal, I had not left the city to pursue the birds; instead, I had turned back halfway. I had reached the edge of the city, where sporadic houses drip into the surrounding heath. There, I felt as if I had missed something, and I had to go home. When I opened the door to my room …

It was under the roof; I did not like to have people weighing down the ceiling overhead, thereby forcing me to help bear them. It was a longish room, not very high. From the windows, one could see beyond the edge of the city into infinity. There was also a small room in which I slept and washed. How many lives I lived in that room! They are not to be counted. And what long distances I wandered, through the window and back again. And even if I was fainthearted at times and thought: Now I am tired, I cannot go on, I was never actually alone up there for even an instant. Someone always showed up at the right time. There was a coming and going. Many people came from far away, where they were now living after turning their backs on this existence. But they did not look as if they had traveled a long distance. They were not exhausted, they simply walked in through the door as if they had been waiting there, and now here they were. Several merely went through and did not see me or did not wish to see me. I did not dare address them, for I sensed that they did not wish to be disturbed. Others halted and looked at me, then they too went on. I had to ponder their gazes for a long time. But some remained, sat down with me, and we talked all night long. They did not want to instruct me; on the contrary, they wanted to find out something from me. Incidentally, we did not just discuss serious matters; there were times when we made fun of everybody. I brewed coffee on an alcohol burner, and we sometimes drank one bottle of wine too many. But whenever we had a very important conversation, then it might happen that other visitors joined in, as if they had been in the staircase, merely waiting for the right word to be spoken. There must have been quite a number of visitors. It was like a cornfield that stretches all the way to the horizon and even beyond the borders; the individual stalks could be seen only in front, and the whole field swayed gently to and fro. I believe they came not for my sake, but to listen to the first visitor. They stood around him, as I have said, not always quite distinctly visible. One only knew that they were there. They themselves never spoke, they merely listened. But with what childlike attention they listened, virtually as if for them everything hung on that. And some of the sentences made them blush for joy; the entire room was then bathed in a rosy shimmer. They nodded at one another as if to say: Look, that is the way it is, and a rustling passed through the field. There were some who had as yet left no trace in any heart, because they had not yet managed to commit themselves to existence. For the time being, they were still waiting and listening and hoping.

Most of my visitors, incidentally, were men; but naturally, women came too. I was afraid of some of them; for nothing was to their liking, and I felt utterly worthless. They derisively nitpicked everything, and I was a wayward child. They behaved very violently; belligerently pushing out their chests, they looked down their noses at me. Why, they seemed to be one head taller than I was. I do not wish to denigrate them; they were probably right in some way — otherwise, they would not have come to visit; but they expected something of me that they felt I ought to do, and I was glad when they were gone. Another type was at least equally unpleasant. They softly shuffled in; I believe they wore slippers instead of shoes. Their faces were somewhat bloated; they had bags under their eyes and slack chins; their flesh was pale and spongy; their movements were weary and their voices soporific. Actually, they only sighed. It was hard to get rid of them once they settled down in the room. But the one I hated most was a little old woman; sometimes, she drove me out of the room, and I preferred walking the streets at night. Upon returning home at dawn, I first peered through the door crack to see if she was still there. She always spoke to me from below; there was a kink in her neck like in a snake's, and her head tilted slightly to one side. This was meant to look friendly, and indeed, according to their external meaning, her words were very friendly and concerned. But there was nothing more venomous.

All the other women, nicer and younger ones, were likewise very earnest. I do not mean that frivolous and coquettish creatures should have come. But why not some who were quite simply cheerful? They also spoke a lot less than the men; hence, it is not fair to call women chatterboxes. One should not listen too closely to the superficial sounds; the blabbering conceals taciturnity. They stood at the table, feeling an object, smoothing out the tablecloth. Then they said: "Well?" And when I asked them to have a seat, they sat down and waited. When I looked up, some were sitting quite unexpectedly at the desk near me. Ah, how long and patiently! And they did not bother me, although their eyes were glued to me. Now and then, a few smiled at me; but there were also times when I had to put down the pen and go over to such a woman, because the one sitting there gazed at me so forlornly that I grew quite helpless. At such moments, it would have been better if one of us had wept for the other. But we men do not allow ourselves to cry and have therefore quite forgotten how to do it. Indeed, we are so afraid of tears that we resort to the most absurd devices to prevent them in women too. That was why the female visitors never wept, although they may have often felt like it, and it would have been beneficial for both sides. So I could think of nothing else than to stroke the sad woman's hair and ask her to spend the night with me. Then we embraced; not out of love, but because we did not know what to do. However, this seldom happened. When I awoke in the morning, they had long since left me without waking me up. But the imprint of their sorrow remained next to me in the pillows, and the smell of those women clung to me so strongly that I was certain the people in the street or on the train that I rode to the city must have noticed it.

Once there was a very young girl present, she could have been barely fourteen years old. Although it must have been winter, she was wearing a kind of shirt of very fine material, which reached down to her bare feet. She warmed her hands at the stove; the heat radiating from the stove door shone right through them. The line of the back of her neck and the tiny hairs also shone. My heart quivered with tenderness. I do not know what she was after. I did not dare to ask; for she would certainly have been frightened. Besides, it was enough that she was warming herself.

Incidentally, it now occurs to me that the male visitors and the women never arrived together or at the same time. While the two sexes usually strive to get as close to each other as possible, trying to abolish the difference, these people showed no such yearning; they kept apart, as if knowing nothing about each other. Indeed, it was as if they lived in completely different worlds.

I am struck by a terrifying thought. What if my name and my image were still alive somewhere? And my name were speaking to another name at this very moment, and I did not know what? Who says that my name perished? Or else it sits on the edge of a woman's bed, and she is deceived by it? Or is a woman not deceived by such a thing?

How shall I check it? This thought, that there can exist such a world of names, and that it may be more powerful, and that I may be utterly superfluous here, is so terrifying that I dare not speak any further.

But no! I experienced it myself.

When I now entered the room, my father was sitting on the sofa. His head had sunk down to his chest so that his beard pushed up along his chin. The corners of his large, kind mouth drooped wearily on both sides. His lips were arched like the wings of a gull. His hair also stuck out, disheveled. Even now, in his sleep, anxious thoughts moved to and fro along their trodden paths on his high forehead.

I heaved a deep sigh of love and gratitude when I saw him. I closed the door as softly as possible, but it awoke him all the same. He must have been immeasurably exhausted. His eyebrows and the shadows under his eyes formed black rings like the frames of glasses. But his eyes themselves shone like dark, mild suns.

Whenever I met him or he visited me, I always pondered what good things I could do for him, even at the cost of my own life; for I believed that he was not sufficiently respected, indeed, that he was pushed around a bit as if he were in the way; nor did he grant himself what was right. Yet I could never hit on anything that would suffice for this purpose, and so I felt guilty towards him. It was the same now, and I believe he noticed it precisely. He beckoned at me to sit down with him, and he asked: "Do you want to save the diaries?"

Only now did I see that he had read parts of them. He was allowed to do so; for it seems to me as if I wrote them for him. For whom else? And he had fallen asleep while reading.

"No," I answered, "we have to take our chances."

And he nodded at me amiably. Nevertheless, I was slightly embarrassed about the diaries. "Come here," he said. "Perhaps we will not meet again that soon. Who can tell what is going to happen. I cannot judge it so exactly. Besides, none of this depends on me, you ought to know." And I realized that he meant that it depended on me. This was his way of suggesting something to me. He fearfully avoided anything that sounded like a demand. "In any case, let us sit together once again. Perhaps the others will also come if it is necessary."

Ah, I do not wish to say anything more about it. I will later on. Or else not. For what words should I use to describe that afternoon and our sitting together? You must bear in mind that he was my real father. Not the one who has the name of "father" in the lawbooks, because he performed the job of procreating me with a woman (I will have to speak about him too some day); but that is an entirely different matter. No, I was lucky enough to find my real father.

One day on the street. A wagon with heavy brown horses was standing at the curbstone. Thick white tufts of hair fell over their hooves. A man was talking to them and feeding them crusts of old black bread. Then I heard his voice. And I was amazed that not everyone heard it, since he was speaking so distinctly, and it could not be misunderstood. And now I knew that this was my father.

I have not heard him again since the thing that happened. I have listened closely; for I cannot imagine that his voice could have been lost. Perhaps it signifies that I am now to speak like him, and then his voice will be here again. But who could manage to do so?

At the table now, where they thought I was sitting, the question that my so-called friend had asked me was answered by the hostess in my stead.

"Why do you think that we ought to know more about it?" she asked.

I do not mean to claim that he was rattled by her response; he had too much control over his facial features. He stared unswervingly at the hostess next to me, but it took him a remarkably long time to ask: "We?"

It may be that this small word was not spoken aloud, and that the other diners failed to notice anything; why, it may even be that I was the only one who thought that word. I have already said that he knew my thoughts and used to voice them. Very slowly, he shifted his eyes towards me, so slowly that the image of the woman by my side, whom he had been watching so attentively, did not evaporate from his face, and I could still make out her barely perceptible nodding. Then he began to speak in his normal way:

"There are only two explanations for what we have seen today," he said in a glass-hard voice, as if pronouncing an unappealable court verdict. "Either those two ridiculous birds were really here, and (no matter where they come from, however many of them there are, and whatever they can do to us) that would mean that things are possible that, so far as we know, could not be possible. In other words: these would not be things that we see unclearly only for now, but that we will have undoubtedly researched, with gradually increasing knowledge, tomorrow or the day after tomorrow; rather, these would be unknown things that have never been and never will be calculated. And, like those birds, they can erupt into our lives at any time; and all we can do is admit that our knowledge is null and utterly useless. Or else: Those birds were not here in the first place; but everyone imagined seeing them. In effect, the two are practically one and the same; the second possibility may perhaps be somewhat worse. For it would mean that we can rely neither on ourselves nor on that which surrounds us — I mean that which we created, and believe we control, by virtue of our minds; for if we accepted our hallucinations as real, we would devaluate everything that we have previously considered reality. To speak even more clearly: We would then scarcely have the right to call ourselves human beings in the sense that we have previously understood the term; instead, we would be creatures that can transform themselves into one thing today and another tomorrow, all according to the urges of their imaginations. 'Creatures' is already saying too much; we would be merely changing manifestations of that boundless drive."

No one interrupted him; yet, although everyone was listening intently, they seemed to be regarding his statements purely as an interesting dinner conversation and waiting for a witty conclusion. Otherwise they would have had to be frightened.

"And toward which view do *you* lean?" the hostess asked, and her words were like a warm breath.

"As bizarre as it may sound, my dear…" he replied. But the name? He must have used a name? "I believe that we are dealing with a hallucination. What puzzles me most is that, according to the clocks, this event can have lasted barely a second. My watch is still running. I wound it last night before going to bed. The timepieces of our male and female friends are still running steadfastly. The same holds for the church clocks. And they all tell the same time. What can be more conscientious than a clock? How praiseworthy of us to have invented and constructed the clock! And now we are supposed to assume that clocks, the sun, and our heartbeat came to a pause, during which the notion of time was suspended? A pause? A moment of unconsciousness? And how long did that pause go on, we must instantly ask. We have no choice. What if this pause lasted longer than time? But that is unthinkable. And how are we to behave after that pause? Why, that would spell despair for many people. I said 'bizarre,' and I mean it as follows" (all at once, there was something tender in his words): "I do not consider myself infallible; but the thing for which I can least reproach myself is that I am easily seduced into self-deception by my feelings and the moods of my blood."

He now raised his glass, in which the evening sun was glowing through the red wine, and he drank to the hostess's health.

But then he continued in an ominous tone: "If I therefore have to admit that I too am prey to hallucinations, then this should alter nothing in my conduct. Instead of pursuing the unknown and thereby confirming it, it is better to explore ourselves, which compels us to assume that unknown things exist. The behavior of that old scientist who, upon hearing the news of the eruption of a volcano, promptly hurried over to observe this rare event and thereby lost his life, is, for me, the only conduct worthy of a human being. And I do not wish to discard my habit of being human. If, therefore, a natural catastrophe were to erupt tomorrow — whether a deluge or a collision in space or a disintegration of all solid things, or the transformation of human beings into animals, nay, perhaps into such dream birds as we thought we perceived today — not because I consider it my duty to salvage some of our present knowledge for a future mankind — how would I arrive at such nobility? — but because it is interesting to study the law of the progression of such a deluge and my own concomitant behavior — indeed, that is the sole reason why I wish to survive as the last and only human being. I am ready."

That was a declaration of war. We exchanged looks. How clear and transparent were his eyes, without the slightest warm tinge or dark uncertainty. I was dazzled, and I probed deeper and deeper into his gaze, seeking the bottom of so much clarity. For a long time, I found myself in a vacuum. But at last, I came upon ice. He hated me.

It saddened me greatly. Perhaps I should have avoided it; my father would certainly have avoided it; but I said: "You have forgotten about fear."

"Fear?"

"Yes."

"Are you trying to feign courage by mentioning fear?"

"I simply mentioned it. I do not know why."

"And what is the consequence of your fear?"

"I do not know," I said.

"Could this be possible?" he turned to my neighbor. And then back to me: "Very well, my friend. I will tell you — I, who am not chosen and therefore probably need to be alert, but not afraid of what the choosing has in store for me. The consequence is that it is a lie — the way we sit around this well-set table and act so certain, as if nothing had happened. And the way we are together today for the last time."

After these words, one might have expected everyone to jump up from the table in order to start out immediately and prepare themselves. But nothing of the sort happened. The hand with the opal settled on my hand, and everything remained calm. They joked back and forth about what everyone would do if the Deluge came tomorrow. And eventually, one of the young women said amid general concurrence: "Tonight, I will fix some sandwiches and pack my new dress. After all, we want to look attractive when the time comes."

We had gotten together to be happy.

I often had such conversations with the man who was my friend. Usually, he talked away at me, and I held my tongue. I held my tongue because I always felt that he was right. Often I thought: Why am I not like him? It might be better now too. Yes, I am astonished that he is not here instead of me. After all, everything pointed to his future success. He was bolder and prouder and always stuck to his purpose, while I frequently had no idea what I would be doing from one moment to the next, and I then had an endless amount of trouble orienting myself. Granted, he would not speak like me now, he would find himself ridiculous and poke fun at himself; but, in the same situation, he would not for an instant hesitate or doubt what step he must promptly take as the most necessary.

However, *he* perished, and I stand here. I probably always knew that he would perish. That was why I loved him, and he hated me.

For when I held my tongue while he spoke, he mistook my silence for scorn and grew even sharper in his formulations. He simply would not believe me when I agreed with him. He thought I was merely trying to silence him. He viewed me as more intelligent than I am, but he would never have admitted it.

For example, I would never have talked to him about my father, or about the others who sometimes visited me. At the very start, I must have betrayed myself. "How can that be?

The man is dead!" he instantly retorted to my allusion. And when I told him that my father was not dead, he irately flared up: "He died on such and such a date. That can be proved at any time." And he named a precise year. Naturally, I held my tongue; for it was painful arguing about my father in this way. But my friend thought I was making fun of him, and he angrily stormed out.

Although I henceforth kept silent about my father, my friend did not hold back with concealed attacks; I often got to hear: "What does your father say, your father, who is moldering in the grave and, incidentally, is not your father?" Yet I am firmly convinced that he knew my father as well as I did. Why else would he have fought so hard against him? After all, he would not have had to do so if my father had really been dead. Also, my father often sat there when my friend was in the room with me, and he listened to him silently as was his wont. At times he sat quite near him, and my friend was undoubtedly talking not to me, but to my father. Yet always as if trying to prove to my father that my father was not there. Even if my friend did not really see my father — which is possible; for his movements towards him were those of a blind man — he must nonetheless have constantly sensed that my father could hear him.

My father and I had a tacit agreement not to speak about my friend. We treated him like a sleepwalker, at whom one should not shout if one does not wish to make him fall. And indeed, he lived in a very fragile glass envelope. Everything was always bright and clear and orderly. But no light shone on the outside, and that was why when anyone who lived inside bumped into the envelope, he believed there was no outside, and he was glad that he could survey the entire world. Everything is correct here, they said delightedly, and there was no denying it. But if an alien shadow fell across their world, they quickly altered the numbers until it was all correct again. What an effort it cost them.

It was not until the very end that I discussed women with my friend. Actually, it began at dinner, and it could no longer be avoided after that. We should have started earlier; perhaps certain things might then have been avoided. In this respect, we were both dishonest. I do not know what prevented him from speaking about that topic and acting as if women did not matter. I, for my part, held my tongue, because I would have been embarrassed if he had categorized them under numbers and concepts or even as the object of a physical need. On the other hand, I was not so certain of my opinion as to risk arguing the point.

But not once, even at the end, did I ever mention my mother to him. He would have instantly replied: "That woman does not exist. She is merely the figment of a milksop's imagination!" And I must confess that I tried to believe him.

My mother never came to my room. I do not believe that she even stood outside the door, holding the knob in order then to turn around because I did not allow her to enter. I simply refused to admit it to myself. In this respect, I resembled my friend. I acted as if my mother did not exist.

And therefore, of course, no childhood existed for me. I heard others talk about their childhoods, and I wondered if something like that had not existed for me too. I tried to go back, but never got any further than that wooden arbor which I have spoken about; and by then, I was already a rather fully developed adolescent. My name was already lurking for me in the bushes. But — curious whether I could make as cheerful a fuss about it as others — if I tried to open the door beyond which I suspected the presence of childhood, it was as if people were sitting on the other side, having supper. A female voice whispered: "Quick, put everything away." Someone choked down the final morsel. An astonished male voice asked: "What is wrong?" And the female voice hissed back: "Someone is coming." And then, apparently speaking to me: "Ah, how nice of you to come. Unfortunately we have just finished supper. Perhaps there is a cup of tea left in the pot."

I found this unpleasant; that was why I refused to probe any further. After all, it was possible that they had neglected to give birth to me, and the people found it unpleasant being reminded of this omission. So far, I had gotten along quite well without a childhood, and should it prove necessary, I might be able to make up for it.

It was only that afternoon that everything changed. It was almost too late.

But first, I wish to report a conversation that I had recently had with my friend. I was reminded of it after dinner. Someone had just come up with an invention that people were afraid of. I have forgotten what it was; even back then, I did not take it as seriously as the others did. Like all inventions that people came up with, this one too was suitable for both preserving life and destroying it. One day, when my friend entered my room, he could speak of nothing else. My father too was present.

"You will see," my friend cried, "we will be able to wipe out everything with one stroke." As if he were proud of it. And he actually *was* proud of the power that he thought he held in his hands. Perhaps he had something to do with it, for he had such precise knowledge about it. His habitual coolness abandoned him, and he went so far as to say: "The earth will blaze up. The inhabitants of other worlds will say: Look, a new star!" And he beamed at me in triumph.

"No," I replied, "that will not be possible."

"Why should it not be possible? Just because you do not wish it?"

"Because no creature can kill itself," I said.

"What do you mean?" he asked in amazement. "I can hang myself or shoot myself."

"But you cannot strangle yourself with the strength of your own hands. And if you could, you would already be sick and ready to die, because you would be making the attempt. A tree is toppled by a storm because it is rotten or because its roots do not hold fast. Or people chop it down because they need it. But it does not kill itself."

"I am not a tree," he retorted, annoyed, "still, I will take you at your word. We are sick and rotten, for all I care. But it is an unalterable fact that we are capable of killing all life." And he proved it to me scientifically, and I was unable to argue. Still, I shook my head.

"You do not believe it," he jeered once again, "because you do not want to."

"Of course I do not want to," I confirmed.

"It will do you no good. It will kill you too."

"Perhaps it will."

"You and everyone and everything. There is no way out," he concluded.

But this time I dug in my heels. "You yourself said they will shout: Look, a new star!"

"Well?"

"So they kill merely in order to live."

If my father had not been sitting with us, I would scarcely

have managed to say that. But I did not wish to disappoint him. You see, I figured that he expected this answer from me. I uttered it for him.

Standing alone on the terrace after dinner, I was reminded of my father's eyes, his trustful way of looking at me during that conversation. The meal was over; the others had stepped into the room where I had previously seen the books and the piano. Neither my friend nor that woman was with me. Only a big, brown, shaggy dog pushed against my knees. I scratched the fur on the back of his neck, and he looked up at me in the same way as my father had looked at me when I said: They kill one another because they want to live. Those eyes had so much confidence, they relied so thoroughly on me as a matter of course that I too had no doubts that I had said the right thing. As if those eyes were speaking to me: What can happen? You are here.

Kill! Kill! How many killed people run about and do not realize it. They were killed by a thought or by someone else's wish. No one sees it. Everyone thinks: These people are just like us. They make the same movements and everything is as it should be. How are we to find out what might have become of them if they had not been killed prematurely. Indeed, the murdered live together with their murderers, sitting at the same table, and sleeping in the same bed; for the murderers too have long since forgotten their deeds. And if they remembered, it would be even worse; they would ask perplexedly: Who made me do this deed? And by then it would be too late; the murdered person would not have the strength to say: It is my fault. I disappointed you. They would then run about like spurned victims.

Yes, a little while ago, I had to ponder quite soberly

whether I should not kill. One of the people lying about murmured in his sleep, startling me. I went to him and leaned over him. He was a middle-aged man; perhaps he looked younger than he was. Long thin hair poured, disheveled, from under a sort of cap and stuck to his chin. His face was broad and his nose short and stubbed. Despite his hollow cheeks and the scar deforming his upper lip, his features were soft and vague. Indeed, a bit sinister, for he could have been mistaken for a woman had it not been for his clothes and his beard stubble. Only his hand, which was cramped on his chest, was the hand of a man. Otherwise it was as if this body had not yet clearly made up its mind what it wanted to be. Incidentally, perhaps he would not have made this impression when awake, and perhaps a person is always like that when asleep, because the flesh remembers that it was born of a woman.

And this is someone with whom I am supposed to live. Ah, a dangerous thought! I tried to make out what he was mumbling. I raised him up slightly by his shoulders, but he slipped out of my hands, and his head dropped back into the clay as if he had no bones. Yet, to my dismay, I had nearly tripped over him. I returned to my post and eyed my hands in disgust. Something of the pasty mass of which this sleeper seemed to be consist had stuck to them. I pondered: If he had talked so loudly as to wake the others, and if he had even (for what do I know about him?) announced something of what had existed previously, what should I have done? And if he did it tomorrow? His face was like a barely kneaded, not yet baked dough. An utterly alien destiny could gain control of it, turning it into something that could not be evaluated. It could become a brother or a scornful adversary. But whatever would have become of it, it would not have been itself. Even if he had eliminated me, it would only have been this alien entity, which would have entered the dough as yeast. I was afraid, certainly! But not so much for my sake. Was it to start again with a murder? And would the dough have collapsed after the deed?

My so-called friend, who used to address me as "friend," would not have doubted what to do for even an instant. But I was not my friend. I myself am like this gray, indefinite face. Hardship and this filth, which besmirch us, making us unrecognizable, form a crust that shields our marrows against freezing. That is the only security we now have.

Ah, to think that I must talk about such matters! Perhaps it is hunger that drives me to it, and I breathe poorly because my stomach is empty. I would so much like to think of something beautiful and talk about it. About young girls strolling along the street, arm in arm. They wear new frocks, and their sole concern is: Don't we look attractive? And whoever sees them smiles joyfully and because spring has come. Or about an adolescent boy, who, in feverish haste, writes something that he believes will be an earthshaking opus. And he peers at the sky and says: Let me live until I finish this. And one's heart quivers with anxious delight when one hears this.

However, my character is such that I do not know how I would act if I suddenly found a lone rosebush in this muddy world. It is possible that the old song would come to my mind:

> Oh, why do you still blossom, rose?
> To whom shall I give you today?
> The summer is gone forever, rose,
> I now must think of yesterday.

But it may be that I will tear it off, thereby injuring my fingers. And then I would hurl the rose on the ground and trample it.

As I have said, I was standing alone on the terrace, with the brown dog. Heavily fragrant white flowers were blooming in green boxes all around on the wall cornice. Several belated bees hummed around the flower cups. In the park, opposite, a song thrush sang, a teensy dot on the tip of a poplar, which stood upright like a supple sword, watchfully pointing at the sky. A pair of lovers walked with a rolling gait across the lawn towards the secret bush. Through the gaps in the trees, one could see the other side of the river, which had to be there somewhere, and the dark, distant line of wooded hills, which separated the world from the boundlessness. The sun had just set behind them. A few beams were still groping their way back into the sky, but were caught by a narrow strip of violet clouds, which hovered over the fiery place of the sunset — like the wings of a gull. And a nameless blue-green arched over it. Anyone who could see it as I did, would have had to cry out: Eternal!

I listened inside myself. A female voice was singing in the house. It was a lullaby.

And then all at once, my friend was standing next to me. I had not heard him coming. I winced as if I had been grazed by the shadow of one of the birds that had been discussed at dinner.

"Now they shout: Mama," he said, his head nodding towards the rooms. He gave me a scornful look.

I wanted to place my hands on his shoulders and say to him: "Would it not be better if we talked about it?" I wanted to tell him everything I knew. I wanted to hide nothing from him.

I had spoken about my father and about the others with whom I had been together. Perhaps I would have even mentioned my mother for the first time. That was how shaken I was when I saw him standing before me and I already knew precisely how he would die. It appeared to be my final chance to save him and to prevent what was to come about. I wanted to speak and then leave before he could answer. I did not doubt that he would then go back into the house.

But my hands were leaden and my tongue was lamed. He shook himself angrily and said: "Thank you, my friend! You are very kind."

Then he turned his back on me and left the terrace by way of the steps leading to the front garden. The brown dog gazed after him. Then it looked at me, its eyes asking whether I would follow my friend. Perhaps I would have hurried after him, but then the dog began to wag its tail, and a voice behind me said: "Do you not want to come in? They are all gone. We are alone."

The ethereal blue-green of the sky left me defenseless.

Someone was always there to guide me, and then it was the right path. It was my fault if I paid no heed and tried, deaf and headstrong, to take a different path. But then the man who wanted to guide me stood sadly at the crossroads, watching me go astray. Yet none of them ever reproached me or said afterwards: You see, why did you not follow us. They merely did their job unassumingly and waited for me to entrust myself to them.

Thus, I was also guided by my brother, the motherless one, to my mother. How could I guess that he knew her? Nor would I have ever dreamt that this was necessary. Now, in hindsight, I naturally realize that there was no other possibility.

It all took place that afternoon when I was with my father for the last time. The others, as he had already surmised, came into my room little by little. First my teacher, whom I had not seen for a very long time; for I imagined I had nothing more to learn. He strode in swiftly, keeping his body rigidly erect, although he seemed to be in pain, or perhaps precisely for that reason, so that no one would notice. Only his head stooped forward at a slight angle under the burden of thoughts. Most of the certainties that one believed in rarely stood their ground against his lucid, penetrating gaze. They simply vanished, and that was why he initially radiated an icy emptiness. Yet his gaze was not unkind, and if one entrusted oneself unprotestingly to the blue of his eyes, everything was fine. He was accompanied by a small, ugly puppy, and he seemed very concerned about it. The puppy licked its feet, which it had injured.

After shaking our hands (he did it with a very firm squeeze), the teacher halted at the bookcase and read the titles while listening to us.

The next to arrive was a large, fat man. I could always hear him wheezing in the stairwell, which made me smile. My father smiled too; we could not help it — the wheezing alone made us feel good. And what a radiant smile emanated from the man's beardless face as he lingered at the threshold for a moment, completely out of breath, waving amiably at us. The doorway seemed too narrow for him, and, after stepping into the room, he also filled it out completely. Not because he was so fat, it was really his personality. He moved like a grand gentleman, everything instantly belonged to him, and there was nothing that could elude his cheeriness. Whenever he laughed, it came from infinite depths, and a merry quaking infected everyone and everything — the people, the furniture, the books. One felt like dancing. It was like an overwhelming piece of music.

He tapped my cheeks with his fleshy hand as if to say: Do not worry, my boy. And my father cried out to him: "This way, old boy!" and pointed at the chair by his side, where the old boy then settled with a moan. I believe his vision was poor, perhaps he was even blind. But that made no difference; for he perceived everything with his ears.

We waited quite a while, and they chatted — I no longer know about what. I must confess that I uneasily listened towards the door. For I venerated more than anyone or anything the man who was still to come, and I was afraid I would not pass his strict muster. My father and my teacher were also uneasy, although they tried to conceal it. Only the fat man remained calm and utterly sure of himself.

Finally, the man we were expecting came — accompanied by my brother. Perhaps they had first met on the stairs, perhaps earlier. My brother, incidentally, was the youngest of us, even younger than I. To my astonishment, his head was bandaged; indeed, some blood had oozed through on the right side of his forehead. Now I knew he had once been hurt in an accident; but that was a long time ago, and he usually did not wear a bandage. So he must have been injured again, or else the old wound had broken open.

I was always very worried about him. He would easily get enthusiastic about something, but was just as quickly disappointed, and it was to be feared that some day, the wrong word, randomly spoken, might reduce him to despair. No one knew better than I how much tender shyness was meant to be disguised by his somewhat eccentric behavior, and what unsated hunger for life was masked by the cynical curl of his lips. So he did not care if from one minute to the next he did the exact opposite of what he had only just claimed in all earnestness; and if people then felt shocked, he would even jeer at them. That was how I had first met him. He had been sitting in a restaurant garden with a number of students, entertaining them with his jokes. The students were fairly drunk and they guffawed at what he said. Incidentally, he too was a student in those days. I was sitting at the next table and I had noticed that he glanced at me several times as if trying to determine whether I was laughing too. Finally, since the noise was becoming too much for me, I stood up, paid, and left the restaurant. At the exit from the garden, he was suddenly at my side, and without so much as asking me whether I even cared to have him come along, he said: "Those professors try to teach us that those mountains back there and these trees and the gables of the houses and that puddle there, which reflects the stars, and this soft night wind that grazes through the archways, and the laughter that we hear from the meadows — that in reality, all those things may be something entirely different and would stop being what they are if we no longer felt them as such. The people who talk to us like that have their podiums and their tenure; it is easy for them to talk. But what can we go by if we are still nothing?" And as we walked side by the side through the streets of the old town, he spoke to me about those things with such girlish tenderness, as befitted the mild summer night. But he broke off somewhere in mid-sentence and said, as if it were the most obvious thing in the world: "Now let's visit the hookers and act like pigs!" And that was where we went. He acted very familiar and exuberant with the girls, and I was eager to see what would come of it. But one of the girls leaned over me and said: "Take him away. It would be too bad about him." I do not know what prompted her; but it dawned on me that she was right, and that no purer boy existed than this one who was experimenting there with indecencies. She had spoken so softly that he could not possibly have heard, and yet he seemed to have: for he took his hat and left the house. In the street, he tried to spit in a virile way and cursed: "God damn it, not even these women know what they are here for."

We often sat up all through the night; I spent most of my time with him. In this way, I casually learned things about him that he would never have admitted if asked directly. If, for example, I had asked him why he acted so nervous, he would have laughed and replied: "Quite simply out of fear! I once met a man in the street, he was so unthinkably ragged and seedy that you simply could not pass him by. Yet his eyes were as soft as a roe's. I happened to have some money in my pocket, so I gave him a little. I also bought him some bread and asked him what his name was and where he lived, so that I could bring him clothing the next day. He named an old-age home in a poor section of town. When I went there, no one had ever heard of him. The administrator said I had probably come upon a tramp and had been hoodwinked. Now that is not so bad. But what I got to see in that home practically knocked me for a loop. Lots of old men who could have been my great-grandfathers were sitting around, waiting for their food. They clutched sticky bowls in their hands in order to receive it, and their conversation went: 'Is there going to be cabbage today or fish soup?' And what a stench and filth, they are not to be described. I was close to vomiting. When they received their soup, greedily making sure that the senile neighbor did not get more, they quickly toddled off into a dark corner to spoon it up. The spittle flowed from their mouths and the snot from their noses. Can one not get disgusted at nature for being constituted in this way? Since then I have been quite simply fearful that some day all people might become like those old men, that they will only lurk for their bad lunch and otherwise stink and be gobbled up by vermin. And perhaps I am to be part of that."

However, I believe that he was just talking, and that this was not the real reason. He had already tried several professions, never enduring any for more than three months. He also kept moving from town to town. At first, when he arrived somewhere, he would say: I have finally found the right thing. And he promptly attempted to convert others to his new position. But all at once, he disappeared; for a long time, no one knew where he was living or if he was even alive, until they finally heard from him. He was an orphan, his parents had died when he was still in the cradle. Some relatives or other must have raised him. I presume that these relatives were to blame. Naturally, it ill befits me to rebuke them; for as a boy, he must have been difficult to understand. But something must have happened at some point. Perhaps at a meal, when they asked him, while chewing: How much longer? And why? And when finally? For I noticed that he was particularly disgusted by people who were having lunch and sating themselves. But I never dared to touch on this issue.

He claimed that I was exactly like him. This was not quite true. However, he *was* my younger brother, there can be no doubt. Sometimes, at the crack of dawn, it would happen that he would go over to the window and gaze out into the uncertain. Then he abruptly spun around, his eyes glowing with faith and pleasure: "Come, let us die together." I admit that he nearly talked me into it. He was like a lover. As I have already mentioned: he had no mother, and that explains a great deal.

However, the bandage he now wore on his head looked good on him; it gave his face a manly touch; why, he looked like a warrior.

He yanked open the door for the other visitor, whom he was accompanying, and, with an angular bow, he ushered him in. He winked at me roguishly, like a grandson behind his grandfather's back.

If I still knew the names of those men, my description of them would not have to be so long-winded. But in this way, I can talk about them with the terms "father," "brother," "teacher," and "old boy," and that may suffice. I also have to mention that it was not I who had chosen them as relatives and models; it was they who selected me to carry out a mission on which they had set their hearts. Almost against my will; for I often yearned to live like other people—that is: without a mission or a mandator. I would then sigh: Why me? Just as they had chosen me, they could easily reject me at any time, if I did not work out to their satisfaction. And then I would have been doomed, since there was no road back to other lives once this road was taken. And resistance was useless.

However, I have no appropriate designation for this last visitor. Earlier, he must have had a very special name, which made it unnecessary to add any essential epithet. I never dared to address him first, even mentally, with either a request or a complaint, much less with refractory words. It was a question of respect. Knowing that he existed sufficed.

So how shall I designate him now? The judge? He was cer-

tainly a strict and unique judge. He stood upright in nothingness like the law itself. As it was later revealed: once, in a highly
critical moment, he had pronounced a verdict that set a uni-
versal standard and perhaps saved the world. However, the
designation "judge" is too narrow for him. "Judge" conjures
up a defendant and the insurmountable barrier separating the
two. But the man I am speaking of was probably very far away;
yet it was not impossible going to him and reaching him,
though it may sound presumptuous to say so. For the difficult
position of judge that was assigned to him had not killed his
humanity, but merely concealed it. As for me, I always called
him the "forebear," and this designation is probably the one
that best suits his character. Only one should not think of this
label as something senile (in fact, my father was older and,
above all, looked older); it should merely clarify his rank and
the degree of respect that we felt towards him.

Everyone turned in his direction when he entered the room.
My father, despite his years, nimbly leaped up from the couch
and strode towards him. The fat man likewise tried to get to his
feet, but, sighing, gave it up and only held his torso solemnly
erect until the forebear had settled down. Naturally, my father
had reserved the place of honor for him, on the couch, but he
refused it and sat down on the most uncomfortable chair, which
was at the table. Moreover, the plaited straw of this chair was
tattered. My father had to reoccupy his place on the couch.
This was quite unpleasant for him, for he did not dare lean back,
he simply sat half on the edge. I myself remained standing the
whole time, as was proper. My brother also remained standing;
he leaned against the wall next to the couch.

They kept silent for quite a while. The fat man had leaned
back in his armchair again, letting out an occasional wheeze.

I was already wondering if they expected me to break the silence. But how could I dare? The forebear, incidentally, had never visited me before; what would have prompted him to do so anyway? However, I had already seen him from afar and I knew that it was he, and that he had to make the decision about me.

At last, my father took the floor: "We have gotten together here in order to ask you to allow him to go to his mother," he said to the forebear, softly and gently.

Previously, I had never once thought about my mother or even remotely dreamt that she was the issue. But no sooner had my father mentioned her than I felt as if I had never desired anything else.

The forebear's face remained motionless. No one could tell whether he had even heard the request. His features were chiseled in stone. His forehead and his cheekbones stuck out sharply. His temples were hollow, and his cheeks sucked in as if from a wasting grief. His mouth was like a line, his lips pressed tightly together; his words were well guarded.

The fat man nervously ran his hand through his sparse hair and cleared his throat. But instead of him, my teacher virtually buttonholed the forebear in an unexpectedly sharp tone.

"I am prepared to act as her defense attorney. I wanted to do so long ago, but I was told it was too early. Very well, it is not my place to judge it. But now it is time to release her from the prison of a murderous name. The verdict may once have been justified — who would dare to doubt it. Her deed aroused such great repulsion and made everyone so profoundly aware of the danger to which the world would be exposed if this woman were still to be given a free hand, that strict laws were necessary to find the beginning of a new road and prevent any relapse. For we were probably by no means certain of our strength and success; otherwise the judgment would not have had to be so harsh. But this verdict was one-sided, like all verdicts. The road that it indicated has been taken, and the result is such that one is now tempted to approve of her deed."

The fat man thoughtfully swayed his head, and my father whispered soothingly: "Not that! Not that!"

Annoyed at the interruption, my teacher continued: "If not that, then nevertheless, none of us now has the right to pass such a judgment as was pronounced back then. This woman was excluded from the life in which she wanted, in her way, to assure herself a share. People did not wish to become guilty like her; they wanted to master their destinies. The attempt was to their credit, but it failed, and we now real-ize that it was doomed, since people went about it with only half their hearts. Destiny was not mastered, it was fearfully locked out. And man, not destiny, was the prisoner of his fear. The unconsumed grew outside the pale of the laws, inside of which people vegetated dishonestly, without warmth or beauty. But the Void attracts Being, and the world of appear-ances is on the verge of collapse."

The fat man nodded, and my father repeated the words: "Without warmth or beauty."

My teacher concluded with these words: "Sons must again be born of mothers, not of slave women. We, guilty of the failed attempt, do not have the right to forgive this woman. For we ourselves are in need of forgiveness. It is our duty to rescind the verdict that was issued under different circum-stances. Let us stop evading destiny."

The forebear still sat there, inert. Only a very feeble twitching of his neck muscles revealed life and participation. It was as if words were attempting to rise from him and were being repressed. His eyes could not be seen, they lay deep in their sockets, concealed under the gray shrubbery of the brows. He seemed to be rigidly staring into space, perusing a text that remained invisible to us.

Now the others likewise spoke about my mother. The fat man, for example, talked fondly about her for a long time, not without accompanying his words with generous sweeps of his hands, as if trying to disperse all qualms. He also laughed in his friendly way; but I believe that, at bottom, he was deeply touched and could barely hold back his tears. His cheerfulness arched across a great sorrow; that was why we felt so comfortable with him, as if listening to some splendid music. The sound of his voice melted even the stone features of the forebear's face, and the creases grew softer, like mountain valleys in spring light. But I may simply have imagined that. "Why bother talking and deliberating so much," said the fat man. "We have done enough arguing, with ourselves and with the world. It would be nice to relax for once." He nearly choked and had to cough. His face turned crimson from the strain. Or was he only pretending he had to cough? I did not dare slap him on the back.

Everyone waited until his coughing fit was over and he breathlessly apologized with a gesture. Then I heard my father say in his shyly suppliant voice: "She is not a bad person, the poor thing. She will be delighted."

Now the forebear finally turned his face towards me. It is not really possible to talk about it and probably not permitted. I noticed that my brother was so agitated that he switched from one foot to the other. In so doing, he banged his head or his shoulder on a small picture hanging on the wall. It seemed to me as if, all that time, it had been rocking to and fro on its nail with a shuffling noise. I cannot say how long it took. I was nothing but the transparent thought of something greater.

"Why is he trembling?" those eyes inquired, imprisoning me in their scrutiny. I did not know that *I* was meant.

"It is not fear," answered my teacher next to me, and only now did I again stand solidly in the room. "It is the shaking of the leaves at the end of the day. It is the uncertainty of a person who does not know his mother."

I glanced, frightened, at my younger brother; for I feared that he would be insulted by that word. But he gave me a friendly smile.

"Why this fear?" said the fat man. "It is cheerful timidity."

"And love," my father softly added.

"What about the grief?" asked my forebear. "It will cause a great deal of grief. But by then, we will no longer be here."

"We have preserved the grief sacredly within us; for human beings did not want grief and they acknowledged only the common plight, which adulterates all genuine things," my teacher replied. "Let us restore grief to them. Then our mission will be accomplished."

"That is it," the fat man added, and he was now truly weeping without hiding it.

"Let it be," my father resolved.

The forebear sat self-absorbed for a while. Then he placed his bony hands open on the table and, gazing at them, he spoke: "Good! *You* shall take him to her, so that he will not go astray again."

He said that to my brother. Then he stood up, and the others stood up too. I have forgotten whether they said anything to me when departing; I was too deeply moved. No, wait: I recall that my father stood in front of me for a while, and we actually wanted to embrace. But we did not do so; it was not customary between us.

Then I was already off with my brother.

Perhaps the person hearing this will be bored and will think: Why does he not talk about the house and the woman he was alone with? For that must be more important. Does he wish to keep it a secret?

I do not know which is more important. Those men are no longer here to guide and protect my life. I do not believe that they are resting; it is not like them. They will be back if the events should make it necessary. But not I will be the object of their concern. Anyone who seeks them will not find them. Anyone who shouts for them or for one of them and accuses them with the cry: Why have you forsaken us? will not be heard by them. The violent shout will return to the shouter and crush him. One can look for the mother and one will find her at any time. But it is different with these men. One has to let oneself be found by them.

I also had to say so much about them in order to explain how it happened that I went to my mother. The one is unthinkable without the other, like that woman, about whom I may be giving too few details. Even if she is less visible, she must be audible to an ear that pays more heed to the sound of words. Perhaps she can be best perceived from my breathing during my pauses and silences.

Granted, it would be nice if I could recount: We walked together through the dining room past the cleared table. She slightly rearranged a vase of flowers, and then we walked on into the other room with the books and the piano. There, we sat down and talked about the evening, using somewhat weary words, and she sloughed off the role of hostess. But I would only be making that up retrospectively.

The only thing that is certain is that I must have been more familiar with that woman than I thought. But I have completely forgotten how that came about. What had previously existed carried, no doubt, too little weight.

You see, I was in her room. It was the same room that contained the mirror that did not render my image, and her bed, in which I dreamt. But now it was night, and heavy curtains had been drawn across the window. When I describe this, it almost seems to me as if she were the same woman to whom I am reporting it all. Only one candle was lit in a white holder, which stood in front of the mirror. The light fell warmly on her face and hands. The rest of the room lay in soft darkness. I too stood invisible in the shadow behind her. For she was sitting on the low footstool in front of the mirror.

I dare not claim that we were in love. Rather, I would guess that the two of us had gotten underway with different goals. We could easily have passed one another by; but we happened to see each other, and we believed that we were the ones we were looking for.

I spoke to her the words that I had previously heard: "It will cause a great deal of grief." Those were not good words on my lips or at that moment. If I truly wanted to avoid grief, all I had to do was leave without first saying that. But in this way, I probably wanted to shed all responsibility, and that was cowardly.

She eyed me skeptically from the mirror. I did not dare emerge from the darkness, because I was afraid she would notice the absence of my mirror image. Since I was standing in the darkness, there was at first only darkness in her eyes. But they stared right in the direction of my voice. Whether her gaze approached me slowly, or I entered it — being curious about whose image was in it, mine or someone else's — then the dreadful thing happened, and I had to defenselessly watch what happened to me. As punishment for my indecisiveness, I became the witness of my destiny.

I saw myself groping through the dripping fog. I was flee-ing the inescapable. I had no idea where I was heading. I kept changing directions. I ran around in a circle. What I saw was not the same man who had so overweeningly bragged that that afternoon, a high-placed visitor in his room had reached a decision about him. Perhaps the forebear had already rec-ognized this and had therefore asked: Why is he trembling?

Now I too saw that I was trembling. I was trembling so badly that it was communicated to the fog around me and to the ground on which I seemed to be standing. It was an awful sight. Nowhere was there anything to lean on. No tree, no wall. All familiar things had dissolved. The world was a clayey ocean. At times, I saw only my head when I stumbled into a trough of the waves, and at times, only my legs, when I came to a hill and my upper body vanished in the haze. That was why I heard myself panting from the strain, and whenever I pulled my feet out of the clay, they made a smacking noise.

Often I halted and listened. I must have noticed what I thought. If only I had paid attention earlier to the small, shy caresses, and not rejected them gruffly. For example, when we sit at the table, facing one another, as we have been doing every day for years now. One brings spoon after spoon to one's lips without thinking of the food. One thinks of the struggle that lies behind one and that is only half completed; and while chewing and swallowing, one already furiously continues to wage the struggle tomorrow. Suddenly, one's hand is grazed lightly. One looks up, astonished, as if the enemy were already here, one sees a smile, the touch lingers on the hand for an instant, but one already angrily shakes it off. And so one day, one stands altogether outside. When the lindens are in leaf, one probably sees it and yearns to be present. But one can no longer find the first word. One grieves, and the lindens also grieve because someone is standing on the side.

Once, a war took place outside. The nations tried to destroy one another. That was a long time ago. The dead can scarcely remember. They tell each other we are better off forgetting all about it, and we will forget it; otherwise someone will feel like trying again and will declare that he has to avenge us. But that is only a pretext, because he is dissatisfied with himself; for we do not need revenge, we need peace. At that time, the storm was raging around the house. The windows rattled, the ceiling shattered, and the tottering walls might collapse at any second, burying everything. But I cried: "Thank goodness! Thank goodness!" and I puffed myself up in defiance. Then someone said to me: How sorry I feel for you. And the ground rocked under my feet.

But now it is too late. There is no more moon, whose dishonest mildness sparks our protest. And we also lack a moonless dwelling. Misery anticipated us and has im-pounded every true haven. We rummage in the garbage cans.

However, I am not blameless in this matter. Why was I not told this by the men who conferred about me in my room? Or did they want me to hit on it myself?

Eventually, I saw myself halting at a precipice. Subsidence

had formed a crater there, deep and with smooth walls. The water had gathered at the bottom, producing a small, milky lake, like a blind eye. Not knowing what to do, I peered helplessly into the depth. Now, I saw a tiny human figure squatting at the edge of the lake. I was so overjoyed that I forget where I was standing; I trod down too hard or stepped forward — in any case, the ground gave way underfoot and I began sliding. Inexorably I slid downhill, faster and faster. It was a highly ludicrous sight — the way I slid and struggled. And someone even laughed. At first, the laughter was remote and alien, then increasingly closer and louder. And, above all, increasingly familiar. It sounded like a friendly jeering.

"Welcome, my friend. I have been expecting you for an eternity," a voice greeted me when I came to. It was my friend.

But how dreadful he looked. In contrast to me, he had always been extremely clothes-conscious. "One makes one's life unnecessarily difficult by standing out against others because of some sloppiness," he had often admonished me. "And we honor the riffraff too greatly by separating ourselves and therefore permitting them to look at us." Yet now he was caked with clay. His left trouser leg was slit up to the knee, the white skin of his shin peeped through. He was wearing only one shoe. It was obvious that he had slid down into this crater just like me. This would no doubt have been the right moment for me to laugh in turn. He even seemed to expect it. But, to his chagrin, I did not do so. I was too amazed. I had reckoned with never seeing him again after he left me on the terrace that evening.

"Did I not tell you that I would survive?" he remarked grimly. "In any case, as you can see, I have not been inveigled into becoming a bird."

I did not understand him at all. But he misread my querying gaze. "Or do you see feathers, claws, and a beak on me?" he inquired mistrustfully. "Why are you gaping at me like that, huh? Do you imagine that you look any better than I? Or do you find it inconvenient to run into me here, my friend?"

Indeed, nothing mutually distinguished us. Each could have pretended to be the other. But that was not what frightened me. "Has something happened?" I asked him.

Now it was his turn to gape. "Are you trying to make a fool of me?" he asked. But since I shook my head, and he also knew that this was not like me, he added: "Where have you been?"

"In the fog."

"I mean before that."

"Before that?" I could really not recall any time in which I had not groped about through the fog. I did not think about that woman and the terrace. Nor did my friend seem to think about them; otherwise he would not have spared me a few sarcastic allusions.

"So you are seriously asking me whether something has happened?" he inquired, still incredulous. "You holy innocent! More, my friend, could not have happened than has happened. If I had not seen it myself, I would regard it as impossible. Or" (even now, he could not refrain from attacking me) "or as one of your fantasies. Yes, it was worth experiencing. Damn you, it was worth it. But what is this? We are sitting here in this mucky hole as if it were the most natural thing in the world, and you ask whether something has happened?" he resumed. "Do you not know that we are all that has remained?"

"What do you mean 'all'?"

"There are no human beings left."

"No human beings left?"

"Now that would not necessarily be regrettable. But it *is* astounding."

"And what happened to them?"

"They have become birds."

"All of them?"

"Most likely all of them. Perhaps some are still left on the other side of the earth, but we need not count on it. Can we even still call this 'earth'?" he cried, smacking his hand on the ground, which yielded like dough. "And the sky, huh? Where is it? Has everything gotten all scrambled up? I would give anything to have one of those boring scientists here in order to listen to his explanations. Not that it would help us much, but it would be quite amusing. My compliments, incidentally, for holding your ground so well. I would have expected you to be the first to proceed to become a bird. Perhaps I would even have followed you for old time's sake and out of curiosity. It was so damn hard anyway not to push off from the ground and fly after the others. What a powerful herd instinct I do have. I had to throw myself on my belly and clutch the dirt. How quickly they all lost their sense of propriety!" he added, embittered. "They even spurt their white droppings about, as if they had never learned to act otherwise. Shameless!"

"Have they really become birds?" I asked once again.

"Do you believe I am in any mood to tell fairy tales?"

"All of them?"

"Yes, all of them. Or have you encountered anyone?

"No."

"Perhaps a good friend will slide down to us."

We both looked up, but there was nothing to see. I asked him to tell me when it had happened.

"Soon after we parted. Yesterday, today, or tomorrow, who can say for sure in this humdrum monotony. I went outside the city. Why should I not go outside the city? I was taking a short constitutional. We had eaten our fill. I see nothing odd about that. I walked all the way to the mouth of the river, where the ocean begins. No sooner was I there, than it started. An endless rustling of wings. At first, I thought I was drunk. But nothing of the sort. One could not be more sober. First that rustling of wings threatened to confuse me. Always beginning far behind my back and then overhead and away. As I have said, it took a bit of doing to keep from losing one's mind. I would never have dreamt that so many people existed. There were also children among them. A few people still found it difficult to fly. They alighted on the shore in front of me, beating their wings and shrieking. And other birds instantly turned back from the swarm and drove the laggards along. In the end, a few stragglers joined in. They circled slowly above the estuary. Fortunately, they did not sight me. Then they too vanished over the ocean, and I was alone. I stood up in order to return to the city. What could have become of it? I do not care two hoots about it. It probably dissolved like everything else. Next, I wandered into the fog and slid into this hole, just like you. A miracle that we did not bang heads in the fog. Well, here we are. You would probably have preferred my taking off with the others, right? But it will not help you. I am still here."

He tried to look at me in triumph, but he failed miserably. There was more query than triumph in his eyes. "Now what do we do next?" He even nudged me with his elbow; for I sat there in silence, mulling over his account.

"We have to wait and see," I responded.

"Wait and see?" he exclaimed, indignant. "What good

will that do? Do you possibly believe that someone will come and pull you out of this hole? Ah, you patient lambs!"

"I am sure we will find a way out," I tried to placate him.

"I am sure we will find a way out!" he mimicked derisively. "Do you know me so little as to think that I have been moping around instead of looking for a way out? Just try climbing the walls yourself. You will not advance two paces, everything is too smooth. And even if we did climb out? What should the two of us do up there in the fog? Do you hope that we will find something to eat? I do not. Or should we now choose lots to decide which of us will consume the other? We used to read about that in books when we were children. And then, if you please, dear friend, the question still remains: Why even bother?

"Why, huh?" he screamed at me. His voice broke. He seemed embarrassed about it himself. "Just look, I have caught cold and I am croaking like one of those birds. In any case," he went on in a calmer tone, "it will be very boring; we have not considered this sufficiently. But what surprises me the most is that you do not seem to find anything unusual about your being in this situation."

"We were alone often enough in the past," I countered.

"But that was our own intention. And if it got too bad, we could go and make fun of people. They were very serviceable for that, at least. But to have to keep staring at one another — oh no, bah!" He spit.

"If you at least were a woman," he then said in a very altered voice. I felt very sorry for him. I did not dare speak, because he would have noticed my pity.

"Earlier, as you know," I let him go on, "there was nothing I gave less thought to than marriage, and I found the idea of children highly repulsive. Not that my taste has changed on this point, but it stands to reason that we have to figure out how to create a bit more life around us. By the way, who knows whether we are still even capable of procreating. Perhaps this fine gift too has been taken from us. It would be worth the try. But for that, we need a woman. If only one of them had been sensible enough not to become a bird. It astounds me altogether: for behind their nonsensical fuss, women generally knew which side their bread was buttered on. Or did you encounter one in the fog, which made you fail to notice all these things, because you were having your fun with her? That would be just like you."

I pitied him more and more. I could not listen to the way he now yammered for a woman while couching his words.

"What is even worse," he continued, "is that we have been deprived of the freedom to decide on our end. How are we to kill ourselves? We have no weapons. This puddle here is too shallow to drown in. The walls are too soft to smash our heads against. There is no place to drive in a nail to hang ourselves from. In short, we are trapped."

"Fine," I pulled myself together. "Let us first look around for a woman?"

"Where do you intend to find one?" he quickly broke in. "Did you see it too?"

I did not know what he meant. He whispered to me that on the way, before getting completely lost in the fog, he had spotted a whole throng of figures on the opposite riverbank. There had also been women among them. Apparently, they had been just as astonished as he to witness that spectacle of humans fleeing into a bird existence. Highly desirous of discussing it with them, he had looked for a bridge. And he had found one. "Heaven only knows how it got there. It had not been there earlier, nor did it belong there. I stepped on to it gingerly. Yes, it held, it was really a bridge. But when I was halfway across, those stupid creatures noticed me and scurried off across a meadow, shrieking all the while."

"Why did you not chase after them?" I asked.

"I will tell you why, my friend. Suddenly, the bridge no longer struck me as being quite all there. And I was right. Believe it or not, the second half was missing, and I very nearly tumbled into the river. Why was the construction not completed? And how did the one half of that bridge manage to hover aloft in the first place? At any rate, I swiftly doubled back."

"They scurried away from you, shrieking?" I asked.

"Yes, they were apparently afraid of me." Then he leaned over very close to me, peering into my eyes. "What is your view of the matter?"

"They must have been corpses," I replied.

He heaved a sigh of satisfaction. "Yes, that is my opinion too. But why were they frightened, those stupid creatures? It used to be the other way around: the living were scared of the dead. But these people seemed to be shouting: Help! Here comes a living person! And why was no one guarding them? We were always told that there was a vicious dog and a ferryman. What terrible lies they always told us, even about such things, yet it would not have been necessary. But no matter, we cannot get a woman from there. And if they were really dead, what am I to do with a dead woman?" He spit again. Whatever had become of his good manners.

I got to my feet. He too instantly leaped up. "Where are you going?" he cried. I am not saying that he clung to me, but he practically did.

"Stay seated here and watch me," I calmed him down. "I am only going over there. The wall looks steeper and drier there. Perhaps the clay is exactly right for shaping a woman out of it."

"For me?"

"Yes, for you." Then I walked around the pond and tested the other wall to see whether the mass could be kneaded. It went fairly well, and I got to work on the spot. I wanted to mold the woman out of the wall. But I was soon so deeply immersed that I would have forgotten all about my friend if he had not drawn my attention by calling to me. "Well, how is it going?" he shouted from behind me. "Will it work?" But I did not reply. I was perspiring from the strain. I wanted to do as good a job as possible.

Actually, he talked the whole time. And no sooner were the first outlines of a woman visible in the wall than he began to criticize me. "Do not make her too big," he admonished me. "Otherwise, she will thrash us soundly. Do not make her legs too short, I cannot stand short legs. Is she going to be blonde or dark? No matter; in any event, go all the way, you might as well make her young and pretty. What should we do with an ugly woman? We have enough of them as it is. Hey, look, her breasts have to be further up." But I ignored him and did what I could.

Then words of appreciation also came from his lips.

"Damn it, you do have the knack. Something is coming of it. She is damn attractive. Do you have some model in mind? Forget it, I do not want to know."

But I stuck to my purpose. I kept molding the woman indefatigably.

All at once, he stood at my side. I was so startled that I nearly botched up my work. There was something nasty in his voice. "Tell me, my friend, for whom are you making her?"

"For you," I answered.

"So, for me? Ah, how selfless!" he jeered. "And what do *you* intend to do? Have you saved something better for yourself? You do not mean to tell me that you are going to leave me this woman and go empty-handed yourself?"

I thought it best to let him speak his piece without my replying. "I have been watching you, my friend," he went on in the same tone. "How you felt her up! Were you thinking of me? Do you believe that this creature will ever forget how you molded her breasts and thighs? Oh, you people! At times, you cannot even count up to three, but you succeed in something like this, of all things. It comes so easily to you people. You know very well that she will run after you like a puppy. These creatures cannot get away from their creator."

"That is not true," I cried out, becoming indignant myself. "On the contrary, they hate him because he did not make them perfect and he knows their flaws."

"But it sounds good: I am making this for you," he kept talking, unfazed. "Thanks, but no thanks! Being dependent on your generosity in this respect does not appeal to me." Turning his back on me, he walked to the other side of the pond. He was truly like an obstinate child.

The woman was completed. That is, she still had to be separated from the wall, to which she was attached through her spine. But that would have been easy to do. Before going about it, I wanted to check my work once again from a distance. That was why I followed my friend.

"Do be reasonable," I told him. "She is not even alive."

That placated him a bit. "Yes, it is ridiculous fighting over a lump of clay," he conceded. "Do you think that she will come alive?"

"It is not impossible. We have to wait and see." The two of us sat down in our old places and looked over at the woman. He kept talking uninterruptedly. I did not care to tell him that it would be better to wait in silence. He would again have suspected something to his detriment.

First he resumed praising the woman, and in rather uncouth words at that. He wanted to hide the fact that he was beginning to like her. Then he racked his brain trying to figure out what to dress her in. "With our rags perhaps?" This brought him back to our appearance. "We are nothing to write home about. I would not be surprised if she rejected both of us. On the contrary, my compliments! What could such ragamuffins offer her." Eventually, he suggested that we should let her choose, and that the rejected one should give his word of honor that he would disappear forever. "He can join the dead. It may not be so bad there, and they are not so far away. As regards me, you know that I always keep my word. Not out of noble-mindedness — this would not get us very far. But for reasons of common sense. After what has happened, it makes no sense fighting over a woman. So, how about it? Why are you reddening?"

I had not been listening, I had been gazing silently at the figure the whole time. It was only this last question that caught my attention. You see, while he was talking, it had looked to me as if the woman were beginning to come alive. Soon I believed I noticed a twitching in her legs, as if she were trying to lift her foot from the ground. Then again, it was as if her chest and belly were rising and she were breathing. One need only have called her by a name, and she would have started walking towards us.

Above all, however, she seemed to be turning rosy. I

rubbed my eyes, and to make sure I was not mistaken, I glanced behind me and above me to see whether the fog had retreated and whether the sun was coming through. But we were surrounded by the same colorless monotony as before.

Thus when I heard the question, "Why are you reddening?" I knew that the rosy glow was emanating from the woman. "Keep quiet and look!" I hissed at my friend.

He looked too; but, unexpectedly, he began laughing cruelly. It was like a murder. The glow instantly vanished.

"You did not make her a navel," he shouted, leaping up. And before I could stop him, he ran over to her.

"How can she have a navel if she was not born of a mother," I called out, chasing after him. But he was faster, and it was already too late. I was only halfway there, then the horrible thing happened.

He stood facing her, stretching out his forefinger to drill a navel into her belly. "Run away!" I shouted, but he was no longer listening. The woman took a step towards him. It looked as if he were pulling her towards him on his forefinger. Then she leaned over him very gradually and with soft movements, first out of tenderness and then as if she were unconscious. The last thing I saw of my friend was the way his hands braced against her, trying to fend her off. But her body fell on top of him, pulling along the entire wall, from which it was not yet detached.

Thus, he was buried.

I did not yet see that the collapse of the wall had created a way out, which would lead to the people, among whom I am now standing. I could not see it because my eyes were confused. I can therefore report no details. Perhaps it is very shameful and ought to remain concealed, so that I need not blush about it in a lonely hour and my weakness need not arouse my false anger.

It may be that I threw myself into the pit and grubbed about in the soft earth in order to dig out my friend. It may be that tears of fright dripped from my closed eyes. And that this ground, on which, standing erect, I was used to measuring my size, yielded beneath me inexorably. Yes, I must have fallen into timelessness. As if the strings on which a puppet moved had all ripped. Nothing was left and there was nothing solid for me to grab hold of. I searched for something familiar that I could join, while simultaneously hoping I would not find it. In the twinkling of an eye, I had definitively sunk away from my past. All the houses, the cities, the countries that I had ever experienced were blasted to nothingness by the whirlwind of my plunge. The earth was merely a nebula through which I fell. I sank more swiftly. The millennia whirled past me like shreds of clouds. Faster and faster. I wanted to scream, yes. I was filled to bursting with a scream. But there was no air for me to utter the scream. I would probably have burst with pain if I had not been finally caught by a gentle unconsciousness that released me from the pain. All I could say was: "I am lost."

But it may also be that I only said this to that woman in whose room I was, who gazed at me from the mirror, and in whose eyes I had to experience all this. I would then have almost been forced to keep talking in an old-fashioned style, the way storytellers used to talk. "And he knelt down before her and buried his countenance in her lap. But she ..." She must have done what any woman would do if something like that happened to her. Such sentences arouse the delight of young people, because they believe that this is what life is all about, and they hope that they too will someday act like that.

Surely I did not kneel down. Yet something similar to what the storytellers mean to say must have occurred. However, be that as it may, a man in shock does not act according to the customs of his time.

At this point, I might pause in my account in order to collect my thoughts, and a few minutes of silence would ensue. My friend (naturally, I mean the one who is gazing at the great nebula of Orion and who was at first very reluctant to listen to me); this — friend would sit down somewhat differently and clear his throat.

"This is a love story," he would say. And since I have probably forgotten all about him during my story, I would not be able to respond instantly to this sudden cry from the darkness. That is why he would repeat: "It is quite simply a love story. And indeed, why not."

"Why a love story?" I would then naturally pull myself together. "Because it happens to include a woman? Or why else?"

"Because you anxiously avoid describing her."

"I cannot describe her. I have explained that often enough."

"You cannot, that is precisely it. Yet she exists."

"You have to express yourself more clearly."

"You do not have to feel offended."

"I am not offended, but I do not understand you."

"The matter is quite simple," my friend would then try to explain to me. "I too once overly prided myself on the statement: I have experienced nothing but myself. In other words: All things and events have no validity whatsoever for me, I am interested only in their effect on me. One day, we are taught that this is a highly unjust outlook, and that other things also have a life of their own, which eludes our perception. The result, of course, is a shock. One is driven from one's fancied center. One no longer dares to say: This is such and such. One grows taciturn. One can only marvel and look. And you yourself know that looking is a suffering, or, for all I care, an experience."

"But why a love story?" I ask in amazement.

"What else should I call it?"

"You could just as well say that I was talking about a woman if I tried to describe a landscape. There are hills and gentle dales in both, and forests, for example, are called the hair of mountains."

"It depends on what prompted it," my friend would continue. "With me, it was not, as you may think, Orion or a nebula; it was a very plain birch that stood in the meadow. How shall I explain it to you? This is precisely the point at which, fortunately, explanations stop. I had the feeling she was watching me. She was thinking something. She may even have been singing. Except that I have no ear for it. Granted, even now, I say: This is a birch. Some kind of word is necessary as a token of exchange. But it is different from before. Perhaps it could also be called a love story in my case. But with you, a woman is the cause, and, after all, we are accustomed to this label."

However, this would not satisfy me. I would object: "Just look around. Look at how thoroughly the world has been destroyed and how wretchedly we live. And you maintain that I am telling you a love story?"

"It depends on the shock," he would reply. "Everyone suffers whatever a thing suffers. The waves continue and are hurled back. We know that from physics. However, I see that I really should not have interrupted you. Please go on. Tell me what happened with your mother; for that is the issue most likely. When did you go to her?"

"Right now."

"What do you mean, right now? I thought you were now with that woman?"

"Yes, that is so."

"Well?"

"I do not understand your question?"

"I asked: When did you go to your mother?"

"Now and then."

"Listen. I realize you cannot tell me everything. Nor is it necessary. Still you cannot tell me that in the situation in which the two of you are, you can go to your mother now and then."

"Why not?"

"You cannot simply say to her: Wait a moment. I will be right back. I only have to settle the matter with my mother."

"Why not?"

"Because I doubt whether any woman would agree to that."

"But this woman says: Go ahead."

"Ah?"

"For perhaps she sets some store by it herself."

"Ah?"

"And perhaps it is not possible without her."

"Ah?"

"And perhaps it is not a love story after all," I would, in conclusion, not be able to refrain from retorting to those three incredible "Ah"s. For he may have a better inkling of a birch than I, and in regard to the constellations, he probably knows many things that are unfamiliar to me. But as far as the love story goes, it would probably be better if I asked not him, but the woman I mentioned at the beginning of this account — I mean the woman on the edge of whose bed I would be sitting in order to tell her this. I admit it is hard to sort all this out. I by no means succeed in doing it myself. It makes very little difference whether I sit on the edge of the bed or sleep in the bed, and, being so close to her, I would not be a mystery for any woman. So is it not more or less all the same from where the smile comes that is mirrored in my words for the first time?

All these things shun the harsh words that hostilely separate them. Their ultimate nakedness is shielded from exposure by the tender glow of a pearl that envelops them. But the all-colored ocean mutely surges all around.

Yes, at some point in eternity, I went to my mother. My brother, as he was ordered to do, set out with me. We traveled for a very long time. We sailed across the ocean. We kept heading in the direction that used to be known as north. But it did not turn cold, as we had always heard. It only became stiller and lonelier.

Eventually, we landed in a gentle bay. It was evening, no wind was blowing. "We have to get out here," said my brother, "it is the last place." We went ashore. The place consisted of eight or ten cabins made of solid tree trunks and with shutters on the small windows, which were all closed. Not a soul was living there. Perhaps fishermen came in other seasons or travelers heading for the interior, or such people as my brother and I.

"We have to spend the night here," said my brother. We walked all the way to the last cabin; removing the key from under the stone threshold, he unlocked the door. "Tomorrow morning, you have to continue in that direction. You cannot get lost. I have to turn back. I can accompany you only this far. But we will spend this night together."

I heard what he said. I tried to look in the direction in which he pointed, but it had already grown too dark. I could barely glimpse a range of hills in the distance. Beyond them there was a very faint strip of blue light. Nothing more. There were no stars in the sky. I listened. It was so quiet that one could have felt the beating of an owl's wings as noise. But there was nothing to hear.

"Why are you not coming?" my brother called from inside the cabin, and I followed him. He had meanwhile lit a kerosene lamp, which hung over a table in the corner. The ceiling of the room was very low, one could fear banging one's head against the beam. Shelves were attached all around, with tin boxes and bottles arranged on them very neatly. Naturally, there was also a stove. Otherwise, there were few furnishings: aside from the table and the benches along the wall, two large crates and a small closet. And then two beds, in bunk form, as is normal in such cabins.

"I want to fix us some pancakes," said my brother. "We are hungry from the long voyage." He started a fire in the stove. Flour turned up, also a pot containing eggs, and a bottle of oil. My brother duly stirred it all together. I was surprised.

"You must have been here before?" I asked.

"Certainly," he answered, pouring the batter into the pan that had been hanging on the wall next to the stove. I asked no further questions. "You will find knives and forks in the table drawer. Set the table while I fry," he instructed me. "Also, get the two old tin cups from the shelf. Wipe them with your handkerchief. I will boil some tea. Perhaps there is some rum here. The bottle is over there. Smell it to make sure it is not kerosene. Yes, it is rum. It will do us good."

He put the pan with the pancakes on the table after spreading an old newspaper underneath. "We do not have to bother with plates. We can eat straight from the pan. That will give us less to clean up."

"Women probably do not come here?" I asked.

"No, I do not think so," he replied. "By the way, the flour has grown a bit moldy. It is not my fault."

"It tastes wonderful," I praised him, and he seemed glad. We ate it all up. By now, the water was already boiling; he brewed the tea, and poured it into the tin cups. He added a solid shot of rum. It made us cozily warm. But we did not talk much.

"There is also a can of tobacco and an old pipe if you want to smoke. In the meantime, I will make the beds," he said. Opening the crates, he pulled out woolen blankets. I walked around the room, smoking. A few yellowed pictures from magazines hung on the walls. A sailboat; a woman in a dress with a plunging neckline; a city with gigantic buildings and a tremendous suspension bridge. There was also a photograph of two children hanging there; they were wearing dresses with lace panties peeping out underneath. I inspected everything.

"Did you moor the boat tight?" I asked again.

"No one will steal it," he replied. I do not believe that he meant to be sarcastic, but I stopped asking, since I realized he would not be answering the questions that I actually wanted to ask.

"There, now it will be soft enough," he said at last. "This is your bed," he added, pointing to the lower one. But I wanted to let him have it and sleep in the upper bunk myself. We argued about it for a while. "Why make a fuss?" he said. "Think of that stupid old saying: Is it not customary to leave the softer bed to the older brother?" So I gave in. I lay down, and after blowing out the lamp, he climbed into the top bed.

But I was unable to fall asleep. The kettle kept humming for a while on the stove; then it gave up. A log collapsed. Then the cabin became utterly silent. I could not hear my brother breathing overhead. It was as if he were no longer there. But I held my tongue.

Suddenly, there was a cry in the emptiness outside, and a yearning answer from afar.

I jumped up. "What is that?" I asked.

"Those are birds. They cry out so as not to lose one another in the darkness," my brother explained. The cries left me very sad.

"It is very lonely here," I then said.

"Yes, it is."

"And bleak. I saw it before."

"Not much grows here. Only moss. Sometimes it blossoms, that looks quite nice."

After a while, he asked: "Why are you sitting up?"

Mustering my courage, I asked him: "Could we not sleep in one bed this last night?"

"If you prefer that, then I will come," he said. He climbed down from his bed and crept under the cover with me. We had little room, but it was better like this.

"Tell me, brother," I began after a time, "why do they not send you to our mother? But if you find the question unpleasant, then forget it," I added, since he did not answer right away.

"I do not find it unpleasant," he said. "but I have to think about it, so that I will not talk nonsense. That must be it, yes: I am too impatient."

"Do you not regret it?"

"Why should I regret it? I have been granted something else. And since you are going to her, everything is in order. One is enough."

"Do you know her?"

"No, I have never seen her. You need not be afraid."

"But you know about her," I inquired further.

"I know that she exists."

"Have you heard that from the others?"

"I just know it. I have always known it even though I did not care to admit it."

"Then tell me."

He lapsed into another silence. Then he said: "If we were not lying here as snug as twins in the womb, I would not talk about it. I do not like talking about it. You know, brother, I saw the women get pregnant and have babies. But they were reluctant to give birth. We always have to bear the burden, they scolded, and after giving birth, they would quickly dress up and go dancing. They also made it clear to the children whom they had to raise. They went so far as to demand gratitude from the children for having given birth to them. This annoyed me, and I became a nasty scoffer. It pained me because of the children, but I would have done better to hold my tongue. Naturally, they threw me out, that was their prerogative. I jeered at them and lived for myself. I lived poorly; indeed, I had to tighten my belt; and I was also surrounded by dubious people. But I was defiant, and it did me no harm. Then came Christmas. Have you ever seen what Christmas meant to them? I scoffed at that too, for I saw that they were fooling themselves. They exchanged visits, went to church, celebrated, and thought: Now we are good people! But the next day, the fight began all over again. Nevertheless, it was unjust of me to jeer; for they made an effort. And it was none of my business anyway; I did not sufficiently respect their property. So at Christmas, the woman in whose home I had been raised sent me a message. Be in church this afternoon, she notified me, so that you can be with your brothers and sisters. Good, I thought, she wants a reconciliation, and you must not be a spoilsport. So I went there. I sat in the pew with them. I saw them folding their hands. I heard the fine voices of my brothers and sisters, I heard them growing merry with the carols they were singing. The carols were good. As is customary with them, there was a tree with burning candles. And I thought: This is quite a good way of celebrating. There is nothing one could object to here. And it made me cheerful too. When it was over, we left the church and stood in the square outside it. My brothers and sisters stood on one side and I stood on the other side. A fierce east wind blasted between us. Christmas, you ought to know, comes in the middle of winter. Then the woman in whose home I had been raised said to my brothers and sisters: Shake his hand! They shook my hand and said: Goodbye! Then the woman also shook my hand and slipped something into it. Then she went home with my brothers and sisters to celebrate, and I was alone again."

"Was there no father there?" I interrupted.

"No," he replied. "The father never went to church. That is not my concern, he would say. When they came home, he would ask: Well, how was it? It was very beautiful, they would say. And? he asked further. Nothing, they shrugged their shoulders. And he fell silent. He was a man of few words. But why are you interrupting me? I stepped under a lantern and looked at what she had pressed into my hand. It was a five-mark piece. I threw it on the ground. I tell you, brother, it was a very cold winter, and the ground was frozen hard. I also took the word 'mother' and threw it down and trampled it, so that it crashed about and shattered forever. Just look at how my legs are twitching. It is not good to talk about it. It angers me even now. Yes, that must be it: I am too young to be kind. Such boys also have to exist. But now, let us sleep."

I wanted to ask him something else, but I refrained. Perhaps there will be time tomorrow morning, I thought.

When I awoke, my brother was already up. He admonished me to hurry. I was to drink my tea, which he had brewed for me. While I did so, he put the blankets back in the crates.

Then we left the cabin. He locked the door and placed the key under the threshold. I felt chilly. It was before daybreak. The cabins and hills stood hard and plain in the crystal-clear morning air. It was always like that before daybreak on this shore; I did not know this at the time. I gazed in the direction of my road and instantly saw that it was my road. Then I turned back to my brother.

We faced one another. It weighed heavily on my mind that I had not yet asked him about the bandage he wore around his forehead. I felt an urge to say to him: You have guided me through the thicket of times. You have warded off sorrows that were intended for me. But I, who call myself your brother, cannot vouch whether I would recognize you if I ran into you today or tomorrow. And perhaps you deliberately make a face in order to lead people astray, and I am also deceived by the mask. Are you wearing the bandage because of my unreliability?

I also wanted to ask him a question for which I had found no opportunity at night: Tell me, brother, has any woman ever loved you?

Boys that we were! We merely shook hands and parted wordlessly. He walked down the road between the cabins towards the dark bay, and I in my direction. After several paces, I looked back at him. He was walking alone. No one was expecting him, nor did he count on anyone's doing so. But then he too turned around. And lo and behold, my brother had removed the bandage. His forehead shone clear and relaxed, and no scar was anywhere to be seen. Now I realized that he had worn the bandage in memory of his most blissful hour.

Then he vanished from my sight.

I would like to say very little about my road. For those who listened to me using big words to describe the impossible would be bored. Or they would shake their heads and think: What of it?

My road lay before me and I saw it until its end. It led upward through a gently rising valley. The valley was not narrow, and the hills left and right were not high or rugged, but softly rolling. Yet everything was quite bare, dark green and brown. Perhaps there were a few remnants of snow, but it may be that I think so now only because at first I felt chilly.

In back, the valley was closed off by a further range of hills. My road wound and twisted in that direction, ending at the point where those hills seemed to create a small pass. Behind this small embayment formed by the pass, the air was a bit less colored than the rest of the morning. But the nuance barely perceptible. Only slightly bluer. That was all.

That is not saying much. But I always see that road and that bleak landscape. Sometimes in the middle of conversations or in someone else's face or in a woman's eyes. At such times, I cannot help it, I have to take that road.

But that is difficult to say. I can say this much: To see the road and to know that this is my road; I need only take it to the end, and the quest will be over. And to know: it is back there, where the road runs into the pass, back there! Is there a word to depict this feeling? Ah, while merely trying to depict it, I am already taking this road again and not thinking of words. The road sucks me in, and I do not resist. I am completely without fear.

Up behind the pass, framed by the range of hills, the heath lay brown and lonesome before me. Wherever there was a moor, the water glittered glassy, and a rosy haze wafted up from the willow herbs that were blossoming there. Here and there in the plain, lone juniper trees stood like old men.

The road dwindled into a very narrow path through the high heather. It led to a cottage standing by the moor. The roof was covered with straw and reeds and sloped all the way to the ground. The door filled nearly the entire front. Only the bottom half of the door was open; it looked as if the lower lid of an eye had been drawn before the scrutiny of the gaze. A bit of smoke poured from the roof ridge and flowed down left and right. No wind was blowing.

Not far from the cottage stood a mulberry tree. Under it sat an old woman. A cat lay in her lap. As I drew nearer, the cat sprang up and, with its tail raised, it dashed towards the cottage, vanishing through a tiny hole at the foot of the door. Suddenly, the woman's hand, which had been resting on the fur of the cat, dropped heavily on her knee. Thus, she noticed that something was about to happen.

She rose from the rock she was sitting on, and she looked towards me. But she did not register me, she peered through me, and her gaze was only a nonviolent waiting. She was listening too, but I must have approached very silently across the sandy ground. Her nostrils barely quivered.

She was wearing a coarse, plain garment, which descended in careless folds past her feet. Her hair was equally colorless; her eyes too were gray and so was her skin. Her face was somewhat bloated, and the lips looked as if they had been stitched on. Presumably, her feet were also swollen from the strains of life and unwept sorrow. However, she was tall and held herself erect in an imposing manner. One instantly saw that she had once been a great lady.

I did not know her. On the way, I had forgotten why I was coming here in the first place. So now I stood before her, waiting for her to address me. But she said nothing. She merely gazed, sniffing, at where I stood. This made me unsure of myself. I smiled sheepishly, hoping she would then speak. But my smile made no reflection on her face. It hovered helplessly between her and me; I was unable to draw it back. Now I was frightened; I feared that this smile between us would conceal me forever from her. Everything would then have been futile. That was what occurred to me at the last moment, and I said: Mother.

One must bear in mind that I had never uttered this name before. At times, I may have been on the verge of doing so. Also, one or two women had probably noticed it and acted as if I had spoken this name. But it had not been voiced. It was merely a warm breath, hesitating for a second and then wafting by.

When I uttered the name, a flowing quiver ran through my mother. The mulberry tree also quivered, as did the reeds along the edge of the moor, and the blue lilies there swayed to and fro. My mother's pale face began to glow like a sunset. Her eyes grew darker and colored; then they started to shimmer, and the tears flowed uncontrollably down her cheeks, dropping into the dry heather.

I was amazed at the change that came over her: my mother no longer seemed all that old, she looked like a young woman gazing at her sleeping lover; she weeps covertly because he may have to go off to the war tomorrow, and because all security will be vanishing so quickly from her life. She does not care to think about it until daybreak and she presses his head closer to her body.

I very gingerly stretched out my hand to caress my mother's face. I dared not do more than that, to avoid changing anything about her. Nor did I wish to stop gazing at her for even an instant. For it imbued me with such bliss. And I said to her: "How beautiful you are."

Then I had to learn what you, my friend, to whom I am recounting this, have already told me: That looking is a suffering. For I was deeply ashamed of my words and could not then endure looking or being looked at. I had to hide my face in my mother's shoulder.

And you, my friend, may learn from this that this is not a love story that boils down to kissing and hugging and goes no further. The span of life from birth to death may rightfully be called a love story. But what happens when it has found its fulfillment? Do you not notice that I am speaking about the span of life that stretches from death to birth? A span that we know stretches across far vaster spaces and that we normally keep silent about only because it cannot be defined with numbers.

Why then do we begin, right at birth, to scream lamentably for love and death, thereby driving away the memory and the words that could announce those things? For the words of this other life are frightened when they hear us scream. They go down to the beach; there they turn around once again and wait to see whether we are calming down. The sea is already washing their feet; at first, they shudder slightly; then they advance cautiously; and all at once, they throw themselves into the stillness — that primal sound of space, which contains their homeland, which was also ours. But we are left only with the empty shells of words. Infrequently, in quiet hours, we put the shells to our ears and hear the stillness roaring. Then we sigh, not quite knowing the reason.

"Mother, something terrible has happened," I, on her shoulder, talked into her. "I have always acted as if it did not concern me, and as if one could keep on living like this. But this is a lie, and now things have gone so far that I would like to scream. And it may be too late. And everything may be my fault. After all, children played in the sand and with dolls. The girls looked joyously into the morning when they shook up their beds at the window. And youths, shadowed by the blue of the evening, rode their horses, swaying, to water and dreamt about heroic deeds. And then the old people who sat outside their front doors between the flowering shrubs of their yards. All that, mother, is no more. It perished, because I had no real share in it. People will point

accusing fingers at me. And the name that they used to whis-
per only secretly — and I acted as if I did not hear it — they
will now shout it out: There he stands, Death! Oh, Mother,
make me nameless."

She let me weep; for it was her sorrow that I was weeping.

Later, I calmed down. "Let me bring you something to
eat," said my mother and hurried back and forth between the
house and the mulberry tree, bringing whatever she considered necessary. She hurried, not tired or shuffling, but young
and nimble, no different from a girl who, to avoid being
absent too long from her visitor, dashes to the pantry and
brings back something good. "I have no meat here, and also
no wine for you," my mother apologized. "But I have buck-
wheat groats and milk. And also honey; for there are many
industrious bees here."

And she watched me eating and occasionally stroked my
hand. The cat too had been given a saucer of milk. A cow,
chewing its cud, looked across the closed portion of the door.

Thus we lived there, and I thought it would be forever. My
mother said nothing about it, she simply made sure that I
lacked nothing. But one afternoon, I looked across the heath
and was startled. Scattered here and there across the flat brown
surface, the small ponds of the moor twinkled. I saw that
something had fallen in there, shattering in its fall.

It made me very uneasy, but I held my tongue. My mother
likewise said nothing and acted the same as before. But at
times it seemed to me as if a shadow were flitting across her
face from left to right. I held my tongue for six days. But on
the seventh, I could stand it no longer and I said: "Mother, I
must leave tomorrow."

"Yes, I know," she answered.

"Do not think, Mother, that I am unsatisfied. It is better here with you than anywhere else. But I must leave."

"I know," she merely repeated.

"I will also catch a new moon for you so that you may enjoy it," I said. "I have seen that the old moon is lying there shattered. This is no loss; it had already become a blind mirror and usually hung in the sky like a rotten pear. But in order to hang a new moon there, I would have to leave."

"I know," she said once again. "Eat now and rest a little. When evening comes, I will describe how it all came about, so that you may know. But I can tell you one thing: Do not scream when you part from me tomorrow. Just think, it is your own will, and that is proper. Do try just once, child, not to scream. Otherwise you will forget everything."

"I will not scream," I promised her.

And I did not scream. But how hard it was for me, it is indescribable. I woke up. I found myself lying in bed in my dirty clothes. It was in the room of the house into which I had wandered when I was returning to the city. Everything around me was dismal and cold and clammy. It was difficult getting to my feet. I kept sinking back. And when I finally got up, I reeled, not knowing why I had gotten up. I stood in front of the bed for a long time, thinking: Should I not lie down again? For how good it is to sleep.

I went to the door and back three times. I held the knob in my hand three times, but could not turn it, and I released it. Eventually, I did manage to open the door, but because of the draft, I did not dare to cross the threshold. Whenever I set foot upon it, I felt as if I were being torn to shreds. I cannot describe how painful it was. It was only with my third try that I managed to get across the threshold. And something ripped. Oh, that pain! I almost screamed. I clenched my teeth. I ran out of the hallway and out of the house and out of the city until I came back to the people among whom I am now.

I did not scream, and that is why I still know everything. But I have to speak about it, I have no choice.

So then listen to what my mother told me:

He did not say so clearly, but he thought it: You exist only because I want to have a son. Let him think that; it would not have really mattered that much. He did not have to know that I had tormented myself for a long time, pondering that I could not lie like that forever while nothing changed. I yearned to stand up, but I could not do so on my own. I need a man (I thought to myself) who would stand up in my place. Perhaps the top of his head will reach the sky. That would be good; I will be glad to obey him. If I had not had those thoughts, everything would still be the same as at the beginning. He did not have to know that.

And I bore him the son. First came your sister, then you, and then two more girls. I was quite content; it was almost as I had imagined it. And for a while, things went well.

One day, he said: "Tomorrow I am going to war."

"Must you?" I asked.

"Yes," he replied.

On the other side of the ocean, there was a great city. The people were more splendid than we. One could see their splendor when they came in their ships to trade with us. They brought things that we did not have. They also looked down at us, it was noticeable. Perhaps they are not peaceful people, I thought to myself, and they may attack us if we do not strike first. That was why I inquired no further. It would have been better had I done so.

In the morning, he went to the ships, which lay ready, and he said: "You are to rule as long as I am away, so that when I return, I will find everything in order."

"Very good," I said.

"And raise the children." You were all standing there. You were not yet grown up.

"Very good," I said.

"And if something should happen requiring a man, then turn to this one here." He pointed to his half-brother, who had been fathered with a maid. The half-brother lived with us in the palace and ate at our table.

"Very good," I said again. Then he boarded the ship. A lot of young men were sailing along to war. They were singing. It could be heard far across the sea. But the mothers and wives were weeping.

For a long time, nothing was heard from the other side. Meanwhile, we lived without the men and kept the house in order. Then a ship came. We were overjoyed upon seeing it; for we thought: Now the war is over. But the order came: Send more young men and ships. It is not so simple.

I carried out the order and sent the men. They too were singing as they sailed off.

The next year, it was exactly the same. Again ships came and took men back. We asked them: Is it bad? But we only had to look at them. One lacked a hand, the other a leg, or else their faces were lumps of flesh. They were also filthy, they spat indoors and cursed loudly when they did not get their way. We had trouble making them feel at home again. They also told us about the many who would never come again because they were lying in foreign soil. Thus our sorrow grew.

This went on for several years. Then came the order: "Send me the eldest daughter. I have promised her to a foreign king, who will be helping us with his people. Otherwise we cannot win." I obeyed. Ah, if only I had not obeyed! The child had grown into a maiden, tall and slender. Everyone delighted in her. I told her to put on a white gown. She stood at the stern of the ship, gazing back. I could not help her anymore. I stared at the white gown for a long time; eventually it was only a dot and then nothing. Weeping, I went home with you from the harbor. You were almost grown up. "What will that foreign king do with her," I said to you. "She is too tender for him." But your eyes were feverish.

Then came the order: "Send me the son. He is now old enough to continue the war for me if I die in battle." Now, at last, I said: No! It is enough! But it was too late. You took your weapons and jumped aboard ship. I ran after you. I called you from the shore. You sat at the tip of the boat, gazing in the direction of the war. You did not sing. And you did not look back even once. When the ship ground away from the harbor wall, something was crushed inside me.

I went home. I did not weep. The half-brother was standing at the palace entrance, and he saw me coming. As I walked past him, he said to me: "Now it is enough."

"Come," I said to him, and he followed me.

I noticed that I was growing old, that was why I took him along. I ignored the two other girls, nothing mattered. They were growing up somewhere in the palace. One of them hated me. Her hatred made her twisted and scraggy. The other one, however, was still a tender blossom, ah.

The half-brother was a strong man. Still, one could tell that he had been born of a maid. His neck was as round as a tree trunk and without the good furrow that you have. One could also tell by the way he walked: he walked through his big toe. But I closed my eyes.

He was very devoted to me, but secretly he thought: One day, I will be king. I acted as if I did not know.

He told me: "On the other side — it is well known — they are wallowing with foreign women in the tents!" And I replied: "Never mind! That is not it!"

Let them have pleasure with foreign women if it does them good. For that was really not it. Rumors passed back and forth across the ocean. Nothing mattered to me. I made no secret of it. You men must have found out about it too.

My mother sighed and kept silent for a while. Softly, I said to her: "I found out one night. They were sitting around the fire. We were standing guard in the open fields. I was lying a bit off to the side, and they thought I was sleeping. They whispered about it. At first, I wanted to leap up and kill them. But I was deeply ashamed and I pretended to be asleep. Now I can no longer be one of them, I told myself, and from then on, I was only like the king's son. The next morning, I had to go to the king's tent to receive his orders. He scrutinized me. If only he does not notice, I thought to myself. Then he looked away and spoke about the war as usual. I peered at him from the side to see if he knew it. But I could not find out."

"He knew it," said my mother, sighing again. Then she went on with her story:

After many years, the war suddenly ended. You men had

destroyed the city and killed all the people. In the east, a cloud of filthy smoke hung in the sky for weeks.

"What should we do?" the half-brother asked me.

"Wait," I said.

Then the ships came back. First it was only like a speck of dust that has flown into one's eye. Then it was like a swarm of mosquitoes on the horizon, bigger and bigger, like a cloud, and finally we could see that those were ships.

"We have to decide," the half-brother said.

"Wait," I said.

I saw that he was afraid. He wanted to run away, but I enjoyed holding him back.

"There are too many of them," he wailed. "Once they are ashore, it will be too late."

"Wait," was all I said. For I knew that they would instantly run to their women and relax. They are all like that.

The ships came closer. The sails were already being lowered. One could hear the screeching of the coils. Then the ships glided into the harbor and were moored.

"Hide in the cellar," I told the half-brother.

"What are you planning?" he asked, hesitating.

"That is my concern, not yours," I told him. He still hesitated. He did not trust me. He thought I was going to hand him over.

"Hide in the cellar!" I snapped. "I will call you when it is time." Now he had to obey me, and he hid in the cellar. It was too late to flee anyhow. I, however, stood with the two girls on the palace stairs, waiting for them to come.

And you men came. The man who was my husband led them. His hair had turned gray and his mouth was creased and tired.

"He had slept on the ship," I interrupted my mother. "'Do not wake me until we are home,' he had told us. I would have liked to wake him earlier; for I wanted to talk to him. I was worried about how we should act when we landed. But I did not dare wake him. He was so tired."

"That was how it was," said my mother. Then she went on:

I greeted him as victor in front of the entire populace, as is customary. He thanked me in front of the entire populace for maintaining the homeland for them, as is customary.

"Are these all?" I asked, pointing at the troops.

"Many have fallen," he replied. He said that they must not be forgotten, and that the fallen would always have to sit at the table with us.

"Why is my half-brother not here?" he then asked.

"He has gone into the city to make sure that no disorder occurs," I replied.

"What sort of disorder?" he asked.

"When soldiers come home, they have a difficult time getting accustomed to peace," I said.

"Very well," he said. "There is no hurry. But I must arrest my half-brother. He did not send us enough men and weapons, as I demanded. This put us in a terrible predicament, and the war lasted longer. I owe it to the fallen to put him on trial. If he is innocent, all the better."

"Do whatever you feel is right," I said.

"However, this will be our last military action," he said to the men. "Now go to your homes and do not forget that we have peace." Then he dismissed them, and the people scattered.

We were still standing on the stairs of the palace.

"Who is that standing by you like a watchdog?" I asked him.

"It is our son," he replied.

"If he is my son, why does he not greet me?"

"Greet your mother," he told you.

"Must you first order him to do so?" I asked.

"It was the custom in the war."

You shook my hand coldly. I wanted to embrace you but you slipped away.

"I sent you a different son," I said to the man. "This is not the right one. What have you done to him?"

"Once we have laid down our weapons, you will recognize him. Have patience with us," he said.

He sent the two girls indoors. He also sent you away. But you did not leave immediately, you remained there, gazing at him. He asked you what you wanted. But you were unable to speak.

"Ah, Mother, I was so afraid for him," I exclaimed.

"I know, I know," she said, stroking my hand. Then she went on with her story:

You were supposed to go to the city, and if any tumult were caused by drunken homecomers, you were to restore peace and quiet. That was his wish. When you still did not go, he said, smiling:

"I can no longer order you. But I can ask my son." Then you went. You repeatedly looked back, but he did not summon you.

Now we were alone. I asked him if he wanted to go indoors and bathe.

"Not yet," he said. "First we want to confer as to whether we can get our destiny to change its mind."

"I do not know what you mean," I answered.

He called for wine, and it was brought.

"Let us sit here, so that the city may see us, and we can be an example for everyone. Soon it will be evening. Let us sit here like two old people who have a hard day's work behind them and can now rest," he said.

"What has made us old?" I screamed.

Suddenly, the daughter who hated me stood in the doorway. He saw that she wanted to tell him something. But he did not want to hear it; patting her cheek, he said: "If we have had to wait ten years, we can wait until tomorrow. It cannot be that urgent." So she had to leave.

"We have made mistakes," he turned back to me, "but we can make up for them if we prevent our mistakes from burdening our children."

"Where is my eldest daughter?" I cried.

"I am not worried about her. When I saw her, I knew that wherever she goes, it becomes brighter," he replied.

"You bartered her to a soldier. He will defile her with his blood-stained hands," I cried.

"I am a soldier too," he said, "but one is not always a soldier. Look!" And I saw him pouring a powder into the wine. "If we both drink it, we will not have to argue anymore. The populace will say: They endured until the end, and when they met again, they died of joy. They will place us in one grave. They will bring the children and grandchildren there and remind them: You must be like these two. Our son will rule here, and everything will have its order."

That was what he said to me, and I understood him precisely. And I shouted at him: "You sold my daughter and ruined her. You took my son from me; for he will never lay down his arms and become my son, the weapons have grown into him. The country is denuded of young men and impoverished by your war. But I was deceived of all happiness. Go to your rest if you are worn out by your deeds. But I want to live and see what I have left."

"Very good," he said. "For the children's sake, it is better for us to be quiet. I will now go indoors, as you wish, to bathe."

I signaled the half-brother, and we killed him in the bath.

Here, my mother lapsed into a long silence, and I too could say nothing. We gazed across the heath, where evening was gathering. We were both very sad. Finally, I heard her voice again:

"The poisoned wine is still standing there."

"Yes, I see it," I said. "It ought to be poured out. Someone might drink it. The children or whoever."

"Let it stand," she answered. "I will watch out."

We lapsed into another long silence. The cat sat a bit off to the side, staring fixedly at something in the moor, something I could not see. I would have preferred our pouring out the wine. I found it unpleasant that it was still standing there.

"You should have drunk of it as he wanted," I said to my mother.

"Do you think so?"

"Yes, it was the only possibility."

"We say that now," she sighed. "But it must have been impossible. Otherwise I would have done so."

"He could also have given me a hint," I cried irately. "After all, I was the son."

"That was why he relied on you wordlessly."

"But he burdened me with it," I moaned loudly. "Oh,

why did I not know that earlier."

"Because you are a man," she said.

"What do you mean? Did the women know?"

"Yes."

"Did they learn it from you?"

"They simply know it," she said. "When the moon changes, we know it, every one of us."

"No woman ever spoke to me about it."

"Because you are a man," my mother smiled. "Not even the men who took care of you and who tried to rearrange the world knew everything. They were good people, I must not say anything against them, and they wanted what is best. But they were only men. You can now see for yourself, it does not last."

I felt utterly wretched. "Oh, Mother, what should I do now?" I asked her. "You are so beautiful that I am astonished, and I would not wish to stop looking at you. But now I am supposed to hurt you. Oh, I would rather drink up the wine."

"Not that," said my mother, holding her hand over the cup. "Before darkness comes, and you grow utterly weary, let me finish my story."

The half-brother said to his men: "Now I am the master!" You see, there were men who sided with him, malcontents, and men who obey anyone who issues orders. He ordered them: "Announce in the city that the war is over because I have killed the man who started it. Anyone who rebels is an enemy of peace."

I wanted to stop it. For I knew that he meant you. "It would be better if we first took the ships," I advised him. I wanted you to have time to flee.

"No, first the city," he insisted.

"The man who has the ships has the power."

"The ships will not sail away."

I could not talk him out of it. He was not that stupid. We argued long and loudly. The guards in the courtyards must have heard us. That annoyed him. "You understand nothing about this," he yelled at me. "You are only a woman. Go inside." And since I would not go, he added: "Now I am the master!"

I believe he would have struck me if we had been alone. While we were arguing, the night descended. We stood in the dark. I looked at the ocean, but now there was nothing to see. We were standing on the stairs in front of the palace.

"Torches here!" he shouted, his voice breaking.

"Why light?" I said. They brought torches; their fitful glow danced red above the courtyard. The half-brother excitedly hurried back and forth. He was waiting for news from the city. I leaned against the wall, in the shadows. The dead man lay behind us, in the house.

Suddenly, there was a shout from the distance: Attention! The shout came closer. Finally, the guards at the gates to the courtyard also shouted: Attention! Then you came. All alone.

"Close the gates!" the half-brother ordered. They did so.

"Seize him!" he ordered further. But this they did not dare.

"Do not be afraid," you said, and tossed your sword over to them. "You can see that I am unarmed."

"What do you want?" asked the half-brother.

"Are you the master now?" you asked.

"I am."

"I do not believe it."

"You will believe it."

"So long as I am richer than you, I am the master. But you

can have my treasures if you wish. I am sick of fighting. You can rule alone if you care to."

"Tell me precisely what you want," asked the half-brother.

"Give me the corpse of the previous master," you said. "I want to sail away with it and bury him where we fought."

"I will never give it to you," said the half-brother. He was afraid you wanted to show the corpse to the populace and stir it up.

"Fine," you replied. "Then kill me. But you will not get the treasures."

The half-brother grew uneasy. One could tell by his voice. "You are lying," he shouted, "you have nothing."

"Do you imagine that we returned like paupers after waging war for ten years and conquering a great city? We have brought back more riches than we ever possessed. One can buy a whole country for them and equip a huge army and wreak vengeance if one cares to. The man who has the treasures is the master. That is the way it is."

"You are lying all the same," the half-brother cried. "Where are the things you are boasting about?"

"Where should they be?" you jeered at him. "In the belly of the ship, of course. You can inspect them first before striking our bargain. But do not think that you can take any of them without me. We are not that stupid. There are several reliable men aboard ship. If anyone attacks it, they will scuttle it. They are scuttling it tomorrow in any case. The dead man ordered us to do so. At daybreak, he ordered, if you have heard nothing from me, then you need wait no longer. The men will obey. We are used to it from the other side. Then you can go diving for the treasures."

I realized it was a ruse, and I was glad. But I held my tongue.

I heard the half-brother grinding his teeth. The gold blinded him completely. He was afraid to make a decision.

"We have time until tomorrow," you said. "For now, I will sit down here. There is no hurry. The night is long." But after a while, you went on: "You are planning to marry the youngest sister. I have heard that you fondle her cheeks in the hallway, like a good uncle!"

"That is none of your business!" the half-brother shouted. I too felt utterly sick. I had known nothing about it. Perhaps you had been told that by the other sister, who hated me.

"It is somewhat my business," you said. "I would rather my sister married a rich man."

Finally, the half-brother asked: "How can I be certain that you are not lying?"

"Send one of your men to the ship," you said. "But he has to take my sword along and show it to them. That is the sign we agreed on. When he has viewed the wealth, as I have described it, he can hoist a light on the mast to let you know. Then they will come and haul the treasures here. In exchange, we will take back the corpse, and you will be rid of us. But if it is not true, then you can have me killed. You are many, and I am unarmed!" The half-brother thought to himself: I will have the treasures and kill him anyway. He is stupid; that was what he thought of you. And he sent a man with your sword to the ships.

"But first put the dead man out in the courtyard for me," you called in order to confuse him even more. "Should I trust you more then you me? Have him brought out. I want him lying here with his weapons, so that he has his dignity."

"Bring him," the half-brother ordered, jeering at you in his heart. We waited. Finally we heard them lugging the dead man. The bier collided with the door-post. They had a difficult time carrying it. He had been a big man. They placed the bier in the middle of the courtyard. You strode over to it and scrutinized the dead man.

"Very good," you said to the half-brother. "It will soon be good when I have buried you," you said to the dead man. "Let us wait." And we all waited.

"What do you intend to do after burying him?" the half-brother asked, trying to outfox you.

"That is my concern," you replied. "Perhaps I will become a farmer and till the soil on the other side. What choice do I have."

"Do you not want to take your mother along so that she can help you?" asked the half-brother. He felt so secure that he was already talking about it openly. He also wanted to look important in front of his men.

"I have no mother," you said.

"What do you mean? She is standing right here. Take a look," he replied.

"That is purely a mirage. My mother was the kind of woman who could not survive the death of such a man. For if she were still alive, I would have to kill her. But she would not do that to me."

"Did you hear?" the half-brother turned to me.

"Yes," I said loudly, not to him, but so that you would hear it. And we continued waiting. How long we had to wait. I believe half the night. It was dreadful.

The half-brother grew uneasy again. "Why can you not wait?" you said to him. "You are waiting for the wealth and for the bride. But I am waiting for death."

Finally, I spotted the light. I was the first to see it, for my eyes were fixed on the harbor. The light rose over the sea like the morning star.

"There!" I cried, and everyone saw it. They joyfully rattled their weapons.

"Soon it will be time," you said to the corpse. I heard it precisely.

"When they come, open the gates and let them in," the half-brother ordered. "But let no one out until I say so."

I listened precisely to the noises from the harbor. All of us listened. We also heard people coming up the streets. They approached slowly.

"Now do you see that I was not lying?" you asked the half-brother and then you stationed yourself by the corpse.

"Not yet," said the half-brother. "First I have to see the treasures."

"Right away!" you said. "Listen to how hard it is to carry them."

Everyone was quite hushed with expectation. But outside the courtyard, the noises came nearer and nearer and the night grew louder.

"They are coming!" the guards finally shouted at the gates and opened them.

The hinges shrieked.

"Is it time now?" I asked loudly.

"Yes," you replied.

I drained the cup of wine. Next, I went to the door of the palace, lingering there. I had to hold tight to the door-post because of the pains. But the half-brother had noticed nothing. He peered greedily towards the gates.

I saw that many soldiers were running into the courtyard. I saw you taking the dead man's sword, which they had placed on his bier, and you leaped towards the half-brother. I went to my room and stretched out on my bed.

For a while, I could listen. First there was a tumult, but not for long. "What is happening now?" I thought. "If only I knew." I listened, I listened. I did not want to leave until I knew. I resisted leaving.

Meanwhile, day must have dawned. I could no longer see it. There were many people around the palace. They shouted: "Long live the king!" And you stepped out on the stairs and said: "Rejoice, the war is over!" I felt very sorry for you. But I had to leave. I was exiled here.

"I am tired of all this, Mother," I said.

"Just sleep, child," she said, "for you must wake tomorrow."

And I slept.

I have nothing more to tell.

I will only say to the people lying around me: Go out there and look for a river. Wash yourselves so that you can recognize one another — for when they see their faces again, they will give one another names. And when the names ring out, the earth will awaken and think: Now I must let flowers and trees grow.

I would also like to tell them: One has to thank the women; for they saved us when we were fed up with one another and wanted to destroy one another. But I am not certain of my voice. Perhaps it is hoarse, I would have to clear my throat, and the words would sound false on my lips. I am not used to saying such things.

That is why I prefer standing here in silence, with my back to the city, making sure that no one goes there. This is my task. If I succeed in enduring there as long as necessary, then I will ultimately be granted an immortal name. They will say "the shepherd," and everyone who utters it will know whom he means.

However, I will have to keep an eye on the man whose face I find sinister. Some day, he will try to push me aside in order to go to the city. I could say: that is his business. For if curiosity drives him there too early, he will destroy himself. Yet how much more havoc would be wrought, and everything would have been for nothing.

But perhaps it is unfair of me to be afraid of this danger and to distrust him so anxiously. It is better to believe in his other possibility. For I imagine that some day a child will be born. While the others still stand around the mother, marveling, and not really knowing what to say, he will be precisely the one who suddenly falls to his knees and cries out: Just look, we have a past!

Then it will be as if the twilight receded from all things. They will see again the city behind me and hear the hymns of those who existed before us and who are always around us when we know we perceive them. They will hear the forebear's voice, distinct and infallible, and they will recognize the teacher's male voice because it is sometimes off by half a note. Now and then, my younger brother will mischievously add an exultant trill to the song, and my father will only hum along modestly. Who would want to miss this humming, which links the voices of the others?

However, the master will lead the chorus with huge sweeps of his arms. His joyous bass drowns out everything else and gives the beat. It makes the hills stretch out all around, and the heads of the trees sway in time. But the mother rocks the child in her lap, and again she says as usual: Just sleep; for tomorrow you must wake.

Ah, we will have to wake and keep silent for a long time, until we earn it —

But I ask forgiveness of you, who have listened to me.

I believe it has stopped raining.

About the Author

Hans Erich Nossack was born in Hamburg, Germany, in 1901, and much of his writing was shaped by his relationship to his native city, where he died in 1977. His work was banned during the Nazi regime, and most of his manuscripts were destroyed by the allied bombing of Hamburg in 1943. After the war, Jean Paul Sartre introduced Nossack's work to France. Since then his reputation as an existentialist and a major German novelist has been firmly established. *The Impossible Proof, To the Unknown Hero,* and *The D'Arthez Case* have been translated into English. This is the first English translation of *An Offering for the Dead*.

An Offering for the Dead

was printed and bound in September 1992 by BookCrafters of
Fredericksburg, Virginia. The text was set and designed on the
Macintosh in eleven point Monotype Bembo. Typesetting and
design by Lucinda L. Hitchcock.

The Eridanos Library